LAKE OF FIRE

LAKE OF FIRE

LIONEL HOUSER

CUTTING EDGE

ISBN-13: 978-1-962896-84-9

Published by
Cutting Edge Books
PO Box 8212
Calabasas, CA 91372
www.cuttingedgebooks.com

AND death and hell were cast into the lake of fire. This is the second death. And whatsoever was not found written in the book of life was cast into the lake of fire.

REVELATION 20: 14-15

NOW: PROLOGUE

F EVER," old Byron Vauzy assured me quizzically, "can't be set down as the work of the devil. No sir! At least, not entirely. It may be hell on some, I can't say; I suppose sometimes it is. But as for me, well—I can't deny that it got *me* something of value; it certainly did—the best story I know." I waited, without speaking. I thought he would lift his round red face to a howitzer angle and begin a yarn.

To the telling of the long, sometimes fantastic tales Byron Vauzy spun, this immense shaded porch looking out and down on the River Godawary in the beginning twilight of a blazing Indian day was ideally suited. Listening came to be, in this place of cruel heat, an accomplishment a man could give hours to perfecting, without begrudging any of the time.

His stories were drawn from a memory as deep and rich as an old chamber in an ancient castle. And sometimes he did not tell them, but only began them and tempted us to call for more, as a lovely woman concedes the momentary pressure of a red mouth.

Old Byron vegetated here as he had for two decades past without seeming to grow older, without, for that matter, seeming to change at all. Under immensely broad, fat shoulders he had a short stubby body and short legs that caved comically at the knees. And he had a huge, hairless head with sharp blue eyes like splinters of cobalt quartz.

"You see, it was fever that brought Norris Haldorn down here to the toes of the lower Ghauts. It brought him down here to tell his story, this damned place between the cholera delta of the south and the malaria belt of the north." Byron Vauzy drank slowly from the long gin buck in the pale green glass. Between his sentences you could hear the solemn old clock in the open hallway *tick, tick, tick* with a sound like a parrot regularly cracking hard seeds. Byron placed his pudgy feet, in white socks, on the railing. In his tone I marked a special belligerency, a pointed pugnaciousness quite beyond his usual calm air in beginning one of these sessions. It was plain he was expecting argument. And he ought, on technical grounds, to have had it, for the date he was furnishing for Haldorn's appearance here was two years later, I was sure, than the day on which the world had been told about his death. I remembered clearly the accounts of the murder of Norris Haldorn and the lurid scandal that flamed up afterwards. But I forbore to disagree with him, out of indolence first and, second, because all of his stories were good rich pieces of narrative, and with his later years he had grown a little testy so that a dispute at the start was very liable to send him into a sulking silence. It was, besides, damnably hot. I mumbled into my glass.

Even then I feared he might not go on. With eyes gone thoughtful he sat looking down past the terraces of maize-sowed black soil to the river banks where, at this hour, the nets, vast sheets of cinnamon-colored lace, were laid out to dry in the sun. A cart full of fruit was trundling down the Bund road, drawn by a bony gray ox. Oranges, those Godawary oranges of a burnished flame color, shone in the cart behind the brown curve of the driver's back. Women were dipping water along the stream, their ochre bodies agleam with perspiration. Canaru came out and asked Byron if there were something he wanted, which was his way of reminding his master that the time had arrived to pick the dinner menu. Byron said, "Get to hell out of here," and

Canaru promised he would do so at once and slid back into the dim house on bare feet.

An hour must have passed before Byron said another word. By that time the watery boom and thump of the regular frog chorus had begun its multisonous clamor, with every pond and pool and every shallow saucer along the river's edge serving as theater and amplifier at once for the sad, damp, reptilian racket. This not unpleasant Indian charivari had the effect now of rousing the old fellow from his revery, something quite odd, for it usually sent him into a shallow doze from which he had to be awakened for dinner.

"I've got fever in me. Always will have," he said, with the same sharp bellicose edge on his voice. Nobody, assuredly, would cross him on that; fever he did have in him. "Nobody lives in this damned country but what gets it into his blood. And then he can't live anywhere else without being reminded twice a year that he belongs to southern India. And then he has to eat quinine all day long. But it has a good twist every now and then—fever has, d'you know that? Haldorn would not have come up here if he hadn't had it. He stayed a month, though he hated it. He wanted to go back across the bay to Rangoon and up that filthy Irrawaddy. My God, it's bad enough here but fever rains out of the air in that place."

Tyndale came out then and heard the last few sentences. "Yes, but there's neither money nor scenery in this mad region of yours," he told old Byron, twirling the ends of his tiny mustache while he talked. Damn his hide! That ended the story, for the time being at any rate, because the old man turned a clear purple from his lower eyelids to his chin and argued sulphurously with Tyndale from then until we went in to dinner.

The dispute continued over the dinner table, with Byron resorting continually to the illogical thrusts of the old-timer until Tyndale, in a weird mixture of English and American slang, said, "You're jolly well nuts!" and went off. Byron took a prodigious drink, wiped his mouth and sank back in his chair with closed eyes. But when he was sure Tyndale had gone, he sat up straight and, as if wrath had been brewed in him which had to be used, no matter how, insisted on opening a furious argument with Stanley Hammer on politics. It rarely wanted more than a sentence of assertion to set young Hammer frothing, and so the two of them flew at it with what seemed to be asinine violence, considering the season.

I wandered out and down the steps toward the river through the warm darkness. The moon had a peculiar zinc tone, as if it were a green disc covered with a transparent milky membrane. The earth, so hot during the day that it seemed any more heat would certainly melt it, now swelled and expended invisible flames without itself cooling in the slightest. Sinuous curtains of pure fever seemed to flow out from the ground. The world baked. While the exertion of walking was close to painful, the faint rustle of air about me as I moved was worth all the suffering. To stand still was to become conscious of the utter inability of a human being to go on existing in this gigantic stew-pot. Movement brought a kind of insensibility.

On the river wall, near the quay, I came on Tyndale, staring out at the vast cherry-black tide of the river. In the night, all the undulations that wrinkled its surface were lost except along the sheet of light made by the moon. The man was sunk in profound melancholy. My pity for him moved me to a cordiality that suddenly opened into a surge of genuine sympathy. Geoff Tyndale had had a desperately difficult time of it, making his trading go; he wasn't a remarkably astute bargainer. I asked him if he'd heard Byron Vauzy tell the story about Norris Haldorn.

"Yes; I've heard it," he told me dully. A few minutes later he expanded to a more alert and animated conversation and he returned to the subject himself. "The maddest piece of lunacy possible," he put it. "The old gentleman is certainly dropping into his dotage. And if that wouldn't prove it, the silly things he tried to argue about tonight, would."

The heat increased to an awful incandescence. We proceeded around to the upper road and back to the house where we fell, panting and dripping, upon the wide chairs and desperately seized Canaru's iced drinks. The month was February, but this was the true steaming summer weather. As if it, too, had swelled with the heat, the thought of that story about Haldorn swung ponderously in my head. I had to hear it. I prodded Tyndale and finally he repeated what old Byron had told him. Heard like that, at night, it fascinated me.

Later on I had the story in full from the torn-faced man himself, and it came to this: That Norris Haldorn, who was dead—dead by violence and hence publicly dead—went sailing interminably in a trig white yacht up and down the Irrawaddy, making an eerie round between the coast and Mandalay, engaged in a quest for someone who, so he said, he would inevitably discover.

"Romance?" he echoed, when once I asked him if it weren't true that that was what he really sought. "Romance? Once I did go after her, yes. But it's more concrete now. Romance, for herself, is a sweet woman. She's a sweet woman, long dead. You can succeed in that quest all right, and when you do, when you grasp what you seek, you have a corpse."

There was much more he said.

This, then, is the account I have made of his bitter, tumultuous errand.

CHAPTER ONE

W HEN the fourth month of his enforced travels had passed, Norris had penetrated some distance up the smoky-yellow Irrawaddy, to a little village called Paok-to. The village was surrounded on three sides by sodden rice fields, beyond which rose mountains coated with thick jungle and peppered with those rambling Kyaung monasteries. Priests dwelt there, polite and greedy, who were as willing to rattle off innocuous axioms for outlanders as they were reluctant to be questioned about any of the mysteries they were reputed to understand.

This place in the armpit of Asia—fecund, moistly alluring, poisonous—exercised a malignant influence on all westerners, Norris had begun to believe. There was in its very beauty, in its brilliant bloom, a threat to a man with a white skin; a warning suave and ominous that he was too pale to withstand this iridescent dazzle of colored heat. For all its lurid radiance, it had powers beyond these surface attractions—furtive and inscrutable influences. More than the heat, it was something in the atmosphere, something apparent only in its effect on the emotions and the will.

In the stifling oven that went by the name of bar, presided over by a native who had fled from Rangoon after some difficulty with the authorities over a little matter of a thousand silver rupees, Norris sat drinking. When it is told that Maongno kept no ice in his bar, it may be known what sort of a place he ran. He himself was inordinately proud of it.

Norris alternately sipped the lukewarm drink and raised his eyes to the doorway and the picture it framed—a vista of endless brown and smudged green fields overlaid by steam clouds that looked like cotton wadding and were continuously swelled by the vapors arising from the hot, damp ground.

Aboard the *Troubadour* there was ice; the yacht was fitted with expensive electric refrigeration; Norris might have enjoyed decently cold drinks in its salon, with an electric fan stirring up the air to sop up the rivulets of perspiration. But he chose, obstinately, to come here. The mosquitos were much worse on the yacht, he rationalized. They came here by the dozens but poured over the boat in an unending, voracious stream. The breed that burst from its eggs on the thick Irrawaddy's current was more bloodthirsty, more likely to bear cholera.

Maongno felt himself superior to the Burmese of the district, coming, as he had, from the metropolis. One of the ways he sought to prove this was by the display of a patent insect-killer spray, a display that was as futile as it was enthusiastic since he had long ago exhausted the supply of fluid that came with the apparatus. Now he filled the spray with water. Every ten or fifteen minutes he would seize it and, with a great show of caution and with many elaborate gestures, like a Chinese actor, go about the room on the balls of his feet, shooting the plunger in noisily. Grinning, he would then turn to his guests for applause. When there were no guests, there was no performance. Maongno did not bestir himself when there were no guests, because the insects had long ago ceased to trouble him personally; the pioneers had found his hide tough and his thin blood unpalatable and, in some mysterious way, must have communicated this fact to the late comers, for it was seldom a mosquito lit on him, and when one did, he let it stay until, discouraged, it droned off. Maongno believed profoundly, however, that his sprayer was effective. It was his notion that it operated somewhat after the fashion of the charms the priests sold, except that in the case of the sprayer the benign humor itself was visible in the mist that appeared after he worked the plunger.

There were some Englishmen in this district—planters, mostly, besides the resident commissioner and his secretary—and by their patronage he made what must have been a very considerable living—for him. Recently there had been trouble farther up the river and the Burma Rifles had passed through Paok-to on their way to the hill lands. But, if he had hoped to profit by their visit, Maongno was disappointed because they camped a mile from the town and came through next morning without stopping. One officer did stop, an intelligence officer. Maongno had information that would have interested the officer deeply, but, ignorant of the affair in Rangoon, and so unable to blackmail or bully the barkeeper, he didn't get it. Of this Maongno had been thinking. Now he shook off these morbid ruminations and set in to polish his glasses, though they didn't need polishing. He kept his little black eyes upon his lone customer.

Norris twisted irritably, as if a shrug of exasperation could free his mind of the dilemma that beset him. He couldn't decide what to do about Night Gambier. This brought him back to thoughts of his father.

As one would flip back the pages of a book to find a passage half forgotten, Norris recalled the conversation he had had with his father on the evening he had arrived home after commencement.

His mother had been there, meek, silent, apathetic. Her face had been the color of tea-rose petals that had lain crushed between the leaves of a book for years. Her hands had been folded in her lap. She had not spoken a word from the moment he walked into the room, glowing and enthusiastic, to the moment he left it, cold and bitter. Scenes like that stayed in his memory; he could remember small, almost unimportant details. His mother had been wearing a gardenia at the shoulder of a formal, silvery evening gown. The cloying scent of gardenias always brought back that scene with terrible clarity.

Norris had seen little of his father ... hurried visits home between trips and conferences ... visits during which his father, if he happened to see Norris, would pat him on the head and walk off. Norris had spent college vacations at the summer home in New Hampshire where his father never came.

Old Cairn Haldorn had been a native Scot, and he had looked like a clump of Scotch heather in the dusty suits he wore. He had a gray face, under hair that was like a skullcap fashioned of worn towelling, with two flaming dabs of color at the peaks of his high cheekbones. A gaunt, hard man with a disposition like a taut wire.

Cairn Haldorn's success in oil had achieved such proportions that Sir Henri Deterding himself, that swarthy, suave and infinitely cunning Dutchman, had made representations, spoken of merger and purchase. But acceptance of the Dutchman's offers would have meant the swallowing of the Haldorn interests by the Anglo-Indian Shell monster, and Haldorn's pride had scorned that ignominy. Even Deterding, when open warfare had been declared, had been unable to defeat old Cairn Haldorn, and finally the two had fallen into a loose sort of anti-Standard alliance except in South America where for every president that Shell bought for petroleum concessions, Haldorn bought a general and a tattered army and overthrew him.

There had been a chill cruelty in the way his father had dealt with him that evening. He could see himself again, a buoyant and naïve stripling, like some new-pledged medieval squire pouring out enthusiastic, visionary plans before a disillusioned old feudal baron sitting in the vast gloomy cavern of his hall.

"I've been spoiling for a long talk with you, Dad," he had said. "I've worked out a lot of ideas that I'd like you to hear, and I'd like you to give me your opinion of them."

"That I will," Cairn Haldorn had grunted.

"I want to go on with my research work, of course—with my studies. But—" Then they had foamed out, his hopes, his faith, his plans … things that, for him, were all light, could never weaken nor die. "I look on my study as only the very beginning. I'm looking forward to things a lot bigger."

His father had nodded. "Little things make big ones bye and bye, lad," he said.

Norris, at that instant, hadn't understood what, specifically, his father meant.

"What I've had in my mind more than anything else, Dad, is doing something in an intelligent way for people who can't help themselves. The rotten living conditions in the city, for one thing. In the tenements. They're horrible. People, human beings, forced to live like pigs. That's cruel and wrong. And I've been seeing a lot of it and reading reports and thinking about it. There's a lot to be done there and the way I've got it figured out is that it's a thousand times more praiseworthy to clean up conditions like that than it is to make more money than you need. And there's the personal satisfaction in doing something decent, something good. I don't mean to be smug or anything like that—but—well, lord—you see what I'm trying to say. I mean bettering living conditions for the poor, giving them a shove upward is … well, isn't it a sort of duty for people like us?"

"Mind your shouting; my ears are still good…. Well, get on, get on with it."

For the first time in his life, he recalled now, he had become conscious of his father as a definite, forceful human being, as he sat there, watching his son with those cold eyes. It had been the first time he had encountered that dry, implacable temper at work.

"Sorry, Dad. I'm letting my enthusiasm get the best of me. And I've hardly begun to tell you what I've got in mind. We can sweep down and clean up the city like a vacuum cleaner. It's going to take organization and careful programs and plenty of money, of course, but I've got the main lines pretty well thought out. Some program, too, whereby we can loan money to them in small amounts, at interest, naturally. That would be only to the families. It's a rotten injustice that thousands of people have to live like animals. Why, some of them don't even know what a patch of sunlight and a strip of green grass looks like. I don't think people who have the privilege of changing that, should refuse it. They do, though. All the time. I suppose you know that better than I do. But here *we've* got the chance to step in and act, without handicaps. The whole plan has been growing on me ever since I took a sociology course that had me prowling through the slums every afternoon.

"I thought I'd work it out in my own mind and then lay it all before you. That's what I want to do, if it takes ten years. Do you see it with me?"

He could see now how pathetically nebulous, how immature and foolish, his plans must have sounded to Cairn Haldorn. The old man had heard him to the very end. And then he had said:

"Ye'll get all that foolishness out o' your seestem. Ah'm goin' to tell ye what's ahead." He had scratched his cheek, holding his bony fingers rigid.

"There's no more o' college, that's one thing. It hasn't done your wits much good, that I can see. Ye may have got a lot o' facts in your head, but ye've tamped in a mighty lot o' foolishness, too. It's turnin' ye soft and ye've had enough of it. Business and life are not soft stuff, and ye've got to make yourself a bit har-r-der."

Norris had started to interrupt.

"Hold yer tongue I Talk when ye've a right to, and listen the rest o' the time. Ah'm givin' ye some sense now, boy."

To Broad Street he was to go, to be a delivery department employee in a brokerage house.

"The motter's all arranged and ye've only to start in," the old man had explained. "And ye can thank the good God it's made for ye like this, so pleasant and easy. Ye'll not have to fight and tear yourself to pieces climbin' up the way your father did."

So many months in the first job, so many more as an order clerk, so many as a statistician. Then into the field service. But not for long. He was to move on. Up the ladder with his father pulling him from above.

Cairn Haldorn had been bound his son should do this. "Ah've respect for your independence, lad. But Ah want to make somethin' of ye. Ye'll get to no place when ye put yourself to wor-ritin' aboot others."

Unlimited funds would still be at his disposal. The yacht would, as before, be at his call. His cars, his horses, his manservant.

"Because your father had to sweat 'tis no reason ye'll have to do the same. Nor wull ye. Ye'll have everything ye've had and more, too."

As his father unfolded the plan, slowly, carefully, Norris began to get angry, but his anger left him when he suddenly realized the futility of resisting this stern man. Rebellion would be an empty gesture. It would simply wreck his own plans. Norris drew a rueful kind of consolation from the thought that he was Norris Haldorn, son of Cairn, and that that same indomitable will must be in him, too.

There had been a good deal, he realized now, five years later, that his father had not unfolded that evening. For one thing, his progress had been abnormally rapid. Within a year, power to which he really had no right hummed under his fingers, and he knew it was only because he was his father's son. As Cairn Haldorn had pictured it for him, it was to have been a steady, plodding working-up-from-the-bottom.

From scattered hints he had gradually begun to understand the darker motive behind the plan Cairn Haldorn had drawn.

It had finally struck him that he was meant to be a sort of glorified showcase for the Haldorn interests; he was to be—was, in fact, already—the social representative of the firm. He had come across a note from an executive in the New York headquarters to a recently-promoted official that spoke of "our own private Prince of Wales; boy, that young fellow is worth millions to us for the publicity and free advertising he gets us, and the prestige. What a front it gives us to stand against in litigation!"

At first he had been bewildered by that statement, but later, when it had had time to link up with other fragments stored in his mind, he had suddenly and fully understood the exact nature of Cairn Haldorn's arrangements. The Haldorn Prince of Wales, he smiled wryly to himself.

When the telegram had come informing him that his father and mother had been killed in an automobile accident, he had been standing in the lounge of the Torregon Country Club, standing before the blue-tinted walls of glass that looked out onto the black-and-white checkered tiles of the swimming pool. His first dizzying instant of stunned disbelief had been supplanted by a strange satisfaction. He had, himself, been aghast at the sense of new power that had spread over him. It appeared to proceed from the knowledge that he was now head of his house.

With a hate fired by long brooding he looked around the lounge with its clusters of wicker couches and red-leather chairs, and out at the men and women—especially the women—with whom he had been forced to associate. The despicable semi-sophisticates; the smug, powdered brats. He detested them. Why, he asked himself fiercely, didn't their parents make them do some honest work, think just one independent thought? Or, he added, why not put them in brothels where their words and, so far as he knew, their actions, fitted?

Now he was done with them and their insufferable smugness; finished with this pretending. He would go back to his studies until he felt that he was ready, and then he would carry out the project he had dreamed of. He was going to destroy city tenements, house people like human beings. And, still closer to his heart, he was going to erect hospitals and vast research laboratories which would operate unhampered, financially. The newspapers often compared the Haldorn fortune to Mellon's, to Henry Ford's, they were fond of speculating on which was the greatest ... so there would be plenty for all the fine things he had schemed.

Then, there was the day he had heard his father's will read, and had realized in what warped, grotesque manner old Cairn had interpreted his son's desires, and what a pathetic, fantastic and monstrous method he had provided for their gratification.

"I, Cairn Haldorn, being of sound mind and body, do declare this to be my last will and testament ..."

For four years he must travel and not approach within a thousand miles of New York, on pain of forfeiting his inheritance.

"It is my further desire and command, knowing well the tendencies ..."

Each year, until and unless married, he must take with him on his journeying, an eligible young woman, chaperoned, worthy to become his wife, meriting the Haldorn name.

"I further direct that should it come to pass ..."

If he should marry at any time during the enforced four-year exile, its prohibitions were lifted—he would be free to return home with his wife without endangering his inheritance.

"I further desire and do hereby command ..."

His companion for the first year his father named in a codicil added not a week before his sudden death. With him he must take Night Gambier.

Bizarre as it was, it was no longer a thing he could draw amusement from. He had grinned and chuckled unbelievingly on first hearing it. He had smiled, thinking of Night. At that time she had been a name, a wavering photograph in his memory, a flash of color—and that was all. As a person, a fellow human being, he had been unable to recall her. Night Gambier, who was nineteen, studiedly insolent of manner, tall and supple, bright ... hair the glistening color of a crocus bud ... who danced with the eerie grace of a leaf of flame, as securely attached to the immediate present as a jazz rhythm.

For a week he had hoped forlornly that Night would refuse to abide by the will of Cairn Haldorn; she was a woman who typified so many things and so many people he disliked. She would like nothing more, he was sure, than to become mistress of the Haldorn fortune. And she had accepted the invitation which the administrators of the will, his father's law firm, had primly extended.

A shamed flush stained his face when he thought of the lewd, sensational stories the tabloids had published brazenly on their front pages. There had been ribaldry and sarcasm in the headlines. The *Evening Mirror* had offered Night some outrageous sum—he forgot the amount now—to write a series of articles. She had refused, scornfully, and the paper had made a cruelly sensational story out of her refusal by printing her conversation, with certain additions and omissions. But her discomfiture had amused him; he had been shrewd enough to say a single sharp "No!" to all such requests and had been left severely alone as a result.

Night's mother was her chaperone. This shrewish flamingo, Lucia Gambier, had driven her husband into an early grave by reminding him every day, and at length, that she had borne his off-spring at the cost of unthinkable pain—undeserved pain— and that nothing he might do could atone for it. Of the two, Norris found the mother harder to bear; her affectation of demure humility, of constant solicitude, was an obnoxious affliction.

Norris Haldorn believed that all comely women, just because they were so, lived to pleasure their bodies. He was unwilling to believe that sex controlled the actions and colored the thoughts of every human. He wanted this distinction among women, between handsome and unlovely, and when Night upset it, she angered him still more. For she had been flippant or bored in her demeanor.

He had lingered here in Paok-to more than a week now, growing to dislike the place as he felt its influence become like heroin upon him. He hoped that this stagnation would provoke the crisis he wanted; hoped Night Gambier would surrender and go home. Then might his sensual self be denied. This frustration would be a small thing to endure beside the fearful confusion that now possessed him. For, seeing her, he wanted her, and, wanting her, he detested her the more, as he saw more and more clearly how she epitomized the life his father had marked out for him. He had come to hate that life as a symbol of his unrelenting enmity toward anything characteristic of Cairn Haldorn.

But the crisis did not come. Night neither surrendered to, nor rebelled against, the stagnation.

"More drink, sor?" squeaked Maongno, bobbing his head on which he now wore a hat like an upturned flower pot. The significance of this headgear was lost on Norris. Maongno was doing him homage; for an ordinary customer he would have worn his old, soiled, pink *gaung-baung*.

Norris shook his head. He did feel, though, like drinking; drinking until his mind went flabby and ceased fretting about this problem. He might, had he been a fool, have made himself believe that he was drinking to ward off the threat of fever. But he wasn't a fool; at least, in the sense that a fool is one who won't, or can't, think honestly. A man can be a romanticist without being a mooncalf, a castle-builder without being a castle-dweller, a day-dreamer without being a dolt.

From some other part of the bar there crept slowly into the room the smell of rotting fish ... fish that was being cooked. The odor drooped under its own weight, would not disperse.

Norris went back again, bitterly, to the beginning. About a hundred million people had read about his odyssey. "Heir to Millions Made Wanderer by Father's Will." So the blatant newspapers told it. Shopgirls and clerks, having propped their morning papers against sugar bowls while they gulped their orange juice and coffee, had remarked that they wished they were as lucky as some people. Imagine! A yacht and all the money you wanted, and a sweet debutante for a passenger. Gosh!

The only legitimate excuse he had for staying on here was his sketching. There were admirable subjects in this dazzling kiln of heat and color. Rangoon had offered little beyond the odorous bazaars, the interminable waterfront and the noisy bars; and *pwes* in Rangoon had been scarce, nor could those few compare with the magnificent all-night dance performances of pantomime tomfoolery here.

There had been a girl—her name was Thayananda—who in a *pwe* a few nights before had excelled in suppleness anything he had ever seen. She had executed a long and intricate dance to the accompaniment of monotonous wailing from a three-stringed fiddle and the piping beat of a semi-circular bamboo xylophone. The significance of the dance escaped him, but he had been absorbed in her poetry of curving motion. Whole families also participated in these performances, entering into them spontaneously, like young animals, with the grace inherited from generations of agile forbears who had danced the same dances to the same minor melodies. But none of the others shone like Thayananda.

Norris, after watching her for hours until she dropped in sheer exhaustion, asked her to pose for him. He was shocked when she appeared with an enormous cheroot stuck in her mouth and a fat, heavy-faced baby at her breast. Her habit was alternately to give the child suckle and inhalations of the cheroot. She would thrust the cheroot in its tiny mouth and hold it there until the child had drawn its lungs full of smoke. She would then withdraw the white tube and pop it back between her own lips. Quaint and picturesque it may have been, but to Norris it only made sordid what had appeared romantic to him under the brassy Burman moon.

The worst thing about Thayananda was her eating. He had looked up from his sketching block to find her stuffing her mouth full of putrid fish. She wolfed it down with audible relish, trying meanwhile to inform him in a choked, unintelligible tongue that the fish was at least a month old and therefore of exquisite flavor.

"You drink now, master?" the unctuous Maongno asked again.

He might as well drink. He had the afternoon before him, it was far too hot to walk and he didn't feel like putting charcoal to a sketching block for rough work, let alone a pencil for fine. Reading was impossible. He had tried to read, found the words without meaning, and usually ended by staring at the face of Richard Todd, suddenly blotting out the words on the page. Todd had been in the same class at Yale as Norris, though he was much older. He had served almost four years in the war with the Canadian forces and had returned to college with a spirit apparently unmarred. Rather, the idealism that shone in his sensitive face had seemed to be intensified. Norris turned down a bid from Delta Kappa Epsilon, after pledging himself to that fraternity, because it had ignored Richard Todd. They had become inseparable; Norris looked on this friendship as the one fine thing that remained of his college life.

Richard was an orphan who had come to Yale on a scholarship. He left, six months later, to go to war and returned finally to resume his studies in the same classes with Norris. A pension from the British government for partial disability carried him through college. That disability, received at Ypres, a triangle of shrapnel in the chest, made it necessary for the surgeons to slice away half of his left lung. He'd suffered harshly in succeeding operations.

Perhaps, if Norris had not turned so fiercely from his father and the furrows his father had plowed for him, moist with Haldorn oil, he would have loved Richard Todd less, for Richard symbolized, in his gentle, earnest way, most of the vague, zealous aspirations that trembled in Norris in those formative years on the campus. Curious, thought Norris, that he, huge, strong and healthy, should be drawn to this weak man, without, at the same time, experiencing any protective emotion. But Todd had once been a brawny fellow, too. Perhaps that explained it. Stranger still, Norris thought, that Richard should be the practical one, and he the impractical. For Richard, with whom he had planned to begin his humanitarian work, had told him to obey his father and postpone their project.

"Nothing founded on bitterness can succeed, Norris," he had said.

Norris picked up his glass and was dully surprised to find it empty again. Was that—let's see—the seventh or the eighth? Or the ninth? He couldn't remember. But bright in his memory was his last conversation with Richard Todd.

They had been sitting together on the deck of the *Troubadour*, talking, between pauses that seemed heavier with meaning than words. It was late—after sunset—but there remained, to warm the sky, a faint afterglow of pale apricot, far to the west.

"It's altogether wrong to run, as you do, to raw extremes," Richard Todd had told him. He had never resented criticism from Richard. "What right have you to condemn your father? Condemn his parents for mating and breeding him if you want, but don't condemn him; whatever he's done, was done as he saw it best. You can't blame a man for that, for doing things as he believes they should be done. That's sincerity. If it isn't, then there's no sincerity at all.

"You've called him a murderer and a despot, and I'm inclined to agree with you on both scores; especially on the despot. But still I don't condemn him unqualifiedly, as you do. Oh, hell, I'm getting so twisted I'd better quit trying to argue with you on that plane."

Norris said, "Argue?" and after that there was a long silence. Richard sucked on his unlit pipe. Later he went to the railing and put his back against it and stared at Norris. Behind him, Norris saw, the waters of the bay were a smooth, unruffled gray. He could remember with precisely what degree of heat in his voice he had said, "I'm out for a good fight every time. You know that, Dick. But with my father it was something different. It's harsh to say, but then the truth is pretty nearly always harsh." Richard withdrew the pipe from his mouth, but remained silent.

"Just this week I was going over some confidential records and there was a report there that had to do with a state in Colombia, an oil state. A little company of Frenchmen were working honestly with the government on it, trying to put through a narrow-gauge. Do you know how Empire went in? First the minister of the interior was lost—ambushed. That was after he'd refused Empire a concession, of course. His successor was beaten to death by hired hoodlums and the third minister of the interior was bribed and bullied into granting the concession and revoking the permit of the French outfit. It was illegal, and naturally the French group went to the courts for redress. Then Empire turned on the local officials and swept through the state with gold. When the Frenchmen won a decision and tried to come back, they were met by a gang armed with machine guns. And the natives everywhere had been turned against them. And on their way back to the capital, on the road, most of them were murdered. It was all there in black and white. Do you want me to—" Richard Todd broke in sharply:

"That doesn't matter, now. You can't right that particular wrong and you won't try, unless you're foolish, to right each specific wrong that your father personally or Empire was responsible for. Certainly there's nothing wrong in spending that money, no matter how it was gotten, on worthy projects. And surely there's nothing morally wrong in your spending it for your own pleasure, when you are forced to, as you are now. The only kind of idealism that won't tarnish, Norris, is a practical kind; I hate to say a thing like that, but it's true. It sounds a lot like a talk one of these sales managers gives to his staff. A lot of drivel about keeping your feet on the ground and your eyes on the stars, boys." A chuckle started up in his throat. "I don't mean that. The trouble with me is, in everything, Norris, that I'm a disillusioned, saddened old cynic who refuses to believe that he's saddened and disillusioned."

They were silent as it grew darker. Richard was the first to speak again.

"Anyhow, don't be worried about money. Somebody always has to own it. It's one of the things that's never free. You might as well be the owner of the Haldorn money else someone who will do only harm with it will have that surplus. Money always belongs to somebody."

What his next remark had been Norris had difficulty in recalling, but at last it came back to him; he'd said, "And that is what makes money—because it has to belong to somebody— like a prostitute that gives a thousand sharp seconds of joy to a thousand men but never bears any children, unless it's more prostitutes."

That idea, Richard had told him impatiently, was rot. "Don't get your young romanticism mixed up with concrete things like wealth. Leave generalizations about wealth to the textbook-makers in economics, Norris. Do you seriously believe that sophomoric philosophy or is it just that you're depressed and upset because you start tomorrow on your odyssey?"

"The explanation's right, but for God's sake don't call it an odyssey."

At that statement, he remembered, Richard Todd's eyes had grown angry. "Take it while you can, boy. Don't manufacture pain for yourself; there'll be plenty unasked come to you later. Be glad."

Out there on the water there had been a sweet tang, inevitably identified with dusk at sea, in the air. He had asked Richard, "While I'm being the involuntary playboy, are you going on with your writing?"

"It isn't a matter of choice; I write ads or I starve." That abrupt chuckle again.

Norris, long ago, had ceased trying to argue Todd into accepting a subsidy and going ahead on his own time writing fiction; he'd even turned down a job in the Haldorn advertising department, a position to which he was legitimately entitled and which he might have held without influence.

"Patrons for creative workers are obsolete," Richard had laughed at him, answering the proposal of a subsidy. "And I make it a practice to be completely modern. If, a couple of centuries ago, you'd been the Earl of Warwick or Lord Liverwort, it would then have been all right for me to have dedicated my humble efforts to you, and to have accepted your money. But not now."

If he were now to offer Richard aid in some other form, Norris knew it would be refused—without rancor, of course, but definitely. Richard would be more grateful for his silence than for his offer. And as for making the trip with him, Todd had long ago refused; and the manner of his refusal forbade further urging.

When they had gone up forward, an hour later, and had stood together facing the panorama of evening sky across the bay, Richard Todd had not mentioned the other phase of this journey, the part involving Night Gambier.

In all the years of their friendship, though they had discussed women in the abstract, women in time, women as social entities, rarely had they talked about women in particular. And yet, Norris knew that Richard Todd had a mulatto girl who served him as mistress and housekeeper in his suburban flat. On first discovering this, Norris had been obscurely distressed, trying to reconcile something that at first seemed offensive in this arrangement with his conception of Todd as a completely admirable individual. Later he had come to believe that there was as much of beauty in the plant Richard tended as in those most other men made to grow. But there never quite left him, after that, the feeling that this device of Richard's somehow separated them a little.

A thin ribbon of silver rimmed the dark disc of the sea. Richard Todd began to sing, very softly.

Look down ...
Look down ...
That lo-o-onesome road
Before you ... travel on ...

To the native melancholy of this negro spiritual, Richard added a note of pathos that made the song a prayer, a prophecy, and a lamentation. At Vimy he had sung it, with a hellish barrage laying its awful bulk down, and a youngster standing next to him in the ooze had gripped his arm and emerged, gratefully, from a dreadful stupor. It was not the words, not the tune, nor even Richard Todd, Norris thought now; it was what you yourself put into all of them. Yet sometimes he doubted this. Had Richard tried, he wondered, to tell him something without saying it too plainly?

And he was just about to ask him then, point-blank, when Todd turned suddenly and said:

"I've always had the feeling, Norris, that the way to reach whatever is God—hold with me, I'm serious now—the only way is to go sailing into an empty sea like that. The only place on earth that's really empty—a sea horizon. Nothing on land compares with it. Every contour ashore is molded in some way by life, even if it's only plant life—but not the sea."

Norris, smiling, had disagreed:

"No matter how hard you try, Dick, you can't make anything fine for me out of this trip. I won't find God out there—even your kind of pragmatic god. No. Not even Eros or Pan or—or Bacchus is out there" and he had instantly been sorry. But it had been said and the best way to unsay it was to bury it.

It was from his dusky woman, Norris supposed, that Richard had learned the wistful little songs he liked to sing. Though these were full of a tender sadness, they perfectly expressed the man's tranquillity, his happiness, his deep and abiding content.

Norris downed another drink, convulsively. Through the doorway, he could see that the cotton clouds over the flat fields had thinned. The sun was beginning to come through.

That night, when Richard nodded a single, final farewell and walked away, calling, "So long, Norris," over his shoulder, Norris was glad, and grateful; not that their leave-taking was done, but that his friend had gone like that, simply, without show or affectation.

"Once again, here," he called to Maongno.

After Richard had gone, he stood there, staring out across the bay, fascinated by the scarlet writhings set up in the water by the light of two red lanterns hung at the end of the pier. The Marin hills and the Berkeley hills looked like cardboard cutouts. The sky was almost a dead black. A lone gull sailed by above him on fixed, unmoving wings. The silence was so complete, he felt that the sound of a handclap would arouse immense and shattering reverberations.

The closing sentence of Cairn Haldorn's will flashed across his mind, like a billboard seen from a fast train. Imbued with a forbidding dignity, the words carried a sting like a curse:

"Obey me not, and suffer. For the judgment of God shall be visited upon the son that hath not the fortitude to go his father's way and, going, hath not the fortitude to do his father's bidding."

CHAPTER TWO

W HEN he thought that that shaggy, weighted sentence had vanished, it was suddenly back again and it seemed, now, to be connected in a new way with the malevolent heat. It lacerated him like a flail, like a lead-tipped whip across his face. It was an incantation chanting him inexorably into hell. It was unbearable. He had to rid himself of it. He stood up; his eyes alone hinted he was close to being drunk. His gait was firm, his tongue obedient. Norris lit a cigarette and strolled out onto the narrow porch.

One of the enormous trading steamers of the River Company had pulled alongside the sagging quay and the villagers were streaming aboard. They swarmed across her decks like ants over a honey pot, to bargain and haggle with the keepers of the shops and stalls. Moving up the path that led to the porch Norris saw Bruce Meterdate, his hands clasped tightly in front of his belly to keep it from jogging as he walked. Meterdate was a planter, a fellow with a complexion the dark red of fish gills. The skin on his face was tight. He made interminable dreary monologues on what he vaguely called "the whole big Indian situation." He came to the bar every day at about this hour. Norris had met him here twice before, and had been forced, against the alternative of rudely walking off, to listen to the man's discourses. Apparently, he lived a solitary life and when he did encounter another white man, made the most of it.

"Hy, Haldorn; have you heard what the damned niggers have done in Nepal?"

Norris smiled vaguely and nodded. He changed his mind about leaving. Perhaps Meterdate's flow of words would help him to forget, would divert his thoughts. He sat down again.

"M-mm a-ah," Meterdate sighed. He put his glass down on the table. Shafts of sunlight kept touching his face. Little beads of liquor clung to the hair-ends of his mustache and, catching the light, glittered like jewels.

"I'm not much of a hand for books, but I tried some reading lately," he announced, as if he were speaking of baked pheasant for dinner. "Couldn't go it. No sense to the thing. Rum book."

"Try another," Norris said.

Meterdate was busy with his tongue, pushing a thread of food from between two of his teeth. Thickly, he said: "Uh, 'm afraid I won't. This one was by—by Huxley, I think it was. Not the main chap though; not the one mixed up with evolution and monkey tails and all that rot. Some other one. Forget his first name."

"I should think reading would be one of the sweetest pleasures of a man like you."

Meterdate shook his head. "I've plenty of thoughts of my own. I don't need to bother my head with other people's ideas in books. Gave this one to my housekeepers. Silly thing it was, too. P'raps they'll sell it to some one. Don't think they can read English. Proper servants. Queer ones, my housekeepers. D'you know that? Queer. Not that I gave a damn." He emphasized his indifference with a solemn waggle of his head. "Lord, no. They *are* funny ones, though. Gone silly on spirits and spooks. A lot of beastly rubbish to me."

He laughed, in his throat. "They're two of the best, though. Say that for them. Two-in-one I call 'em. Pukka good cooking on my table and keep their mouths shut when I tell 'em to. Good cooking."

For no other reason than a perverse desire to irk Meterdate, Norris returned to the subject of spooks.

"So sure there's nothing in what the spiritualists say?"

"Whacking lot of guff. Why, I remember once in Liverpool—" He left the sentence unfinished. Norris asked: "Well, you don't think much of Sir Oliver Lodge, do you?"

This, Meterdate understood suddenly through the agreeable mist settling over his consciousness, was an American asking him, Bruce Meterdate, his opinion of an Englishman. "A genius," he declared ponderously. "Boy, BOY! Liquor here. Both of us. God damn you, hurry up! It's humiliating enough to drink your liquor without having to let our hides rot waiting for it to be served."

What was his judgment of Conan Doyle, Norris persisted.

"Eh? Eh? Who? Conan Doyle? Another genius. Quite. Everybody bloody well knows it, too." He was a trifle aggrieved.

Both of them were talking slowly. "You're ready to grant that men like that have minds a shade above ours—a good bit, in fact?"

Meterdate straightened a little in his chair. "I say, aren't you smearing it on a bit?"

"A bit," Norris agreed.

Meterdate nodded. "Laddy," he proclaimed, bobbing his head loosely, "I'm getting a bit wobbly. Can't say why. Shameful. Never believed I'd see the day I couldn't hold my drinks like a gentleman. I don't feel very tidy."

Norris insisted. "You grant the superiority of such men, and yet you jeer at spiritualism when they believe implicitly in it."

Meterdate weaved around on his chair. He cleared his throat and said *Hmm* and *Arumph* and rubbed his nose comically with the palm of his hand. His mind grappled futilely with the question. At last he spied an escape, sighed happily, poised his glass under his lips, and answered: "My boy, that's religion. I never argue about religion. Mucky business. Every man to his own wants there, I say. Down the gozzle she goes. Have another, won't you?"

They had another, and Meterdate said: "Let me ask you—ask you—wha's use of all this thinking?" He hiccoughed, and looked at Norris with round eyes, as if hurt and surprised that his body, more particularly his diaphragm, should play him such a trick.

Abruptly Norris was weary of the man. Meterdate was going to become maudlin. After shaking hands three times, Norris left the place.

His confusion grew as Norris walked on, head erect, his eyes seeing nothing. His thoughts skipped about so nimbly, so many new ones appearing and disappearing, that he caught only snatches of each, like fragments of half-remembered dreams. Always as a background, like a set scene upon a vaudeville stage before which a dozen varied turns appear, was his perplexity about Night Gambier. Was it vanity or courage that made her continue, that kept her, now, from surrender?

"If we'd been born a hundred years ago," she had said this morning, "and we'd been making this trip across the Alleghenies in a dirty wagon, maybe—"

"Maybe," Norris had interrupted irritably, "you wouldn't have come, eh?"

"I wouldn't have had any choice. Women did pretty much what their men ordered them to do, then, didn't they?"

He had been sure she was mocking him. That she might be here because of some sudden affection for him never occurred to Norris. Vanity, pride, fear—these kept her from going home now.

A hot, dry wind seemed to blow fiercely against his head. He was seized by the ridiculous notion that if he should touch his fingers to his face they would be scorched. It was mad to encourage such notions. Confusion angered and further bewildered him. Out of this mental turmoil a rose the image of Richard Todd. Richard, thank God, was constant and unchanging and satisfactory while all other things whirled and twisted crazily.

Once he thought of Lucia Gambier, Night's mother, a small shrewish woman with a fawning tongue and hard, beady eyes. Norris collided with a native bearing a bale of salmon-colored silk on his head. The fellow laughed joyously as he picked up the cloth. So many things seemed laughable to these dark people. And yet they were so serious about things that didn't matter.

Norris looked around. He was aboard the *Yorkshire Belle* and conscious for the first time of the strange cacophony of voices, shrilling, droning, wailing all about him. He was grateful for the shade. But his face didn't feel cooler; the tumbling flood of sounds here seemed to be generating an added heat. The deck around him sounded as if a hundred phonographs of varying ages, each playing a different record, had been set going at once. The continuous clash of tone against discordant tone dizzied him.

A crowd had gathered about one of the booths; a path opened to its center and Norris, rather than push through the mass of moist brown bodies on each side, entered it. A dumpy native woman with huge breasts that bobbled with every motion of her head and arms, was arguing with a peddler.

"Aya! The size of thy wisdom grows small as the size of an elephant's buttocks grows large," she was shrilling, in Burmese, at the seller of patent medicines.

"Faugh!" the peddler hissed. "Not a penny less is the price, for all thy foolish words." His brew, he reiterated, with a swing of his arms, was a panacea for all ailments, compounded of ingredients both rare and expensive, and easily worth double the miserably small price he asked for it.

The woman had no quarrel with the peddler's claims; even while she argued with him she pointed out through gestures easily recognizable what her trouble was. But she continued to revile him for his harshness.

"I will buy of another whose medicine is better than thine and who has not a heart of stone," she announced.

The dealer shrugged his shoulders. "What is that to me? There is none to compare with this medicine and the cost is now too low."

The government, Norris remembered, had some hand in the operation of these boats. Why, he now wondered, did they permit these fellows to sell worthless medicines? Perhaps it was just as well, though. If they weren't buying this stuff they'd probably be buying amulets and charms from the native priests.

The crowd now began to offer suggestions to the prospective purchaser, for their sympathies were all with her since many of them were attracted, even as the woman, by the potent hue of the medicine and its still more impressive label.

"Tell him we shall bring one who is sick to test his stuff."

"Tell us how much he sold it for to the people in the village up the river."

"Give us then two bottles for what you ask for one," the woman shouted. She was acting as a leader, though not because of her sex, since the men were quite the equal of the women in bargaining, and participated actively and eagerly.

When the woman paused to re-light her cheroot, and the dealer gallantly held the match for her, the crowd broke and thinned out, suspecting a conspiracy. Norris walked away. The noise no longer irked him; it seemed to recede and the dissonance began to smooth itself out.

All at once he was sure he was drunk. It was the first time in his life he had ever seen a concrete thing that proved conclusively to himself that he was crazy with alcohol. Unmistakably, he saw himself standing a few feet away, in a stall where piles of cheap jewelry were exposed in glittering heaps on shallow wooden trays. This Norris Haldorn had his back to the booth, and he was watching the crowd swarm by in front, a discontented expression pinching his face.

Norris stood stockstill, waiting for the other Norris to move. Perhaps, he thought, with the absurd alarm of the tipsy, the other was the real one and he was the fiction. The feel of his bony bamboo cane under his arm, the strong smells, the noise, all these reassured him; it was all right: the other was only mist, a projected thought, a trick his eyes were playing upon him.

And he stood for a long time and stared, entertained by the diverting corollaries of this fancy. He was stirred to elaborate on its possibilities. A name—there!—Freud, occurred to him. This was a dream, a Freudian dream. What if it *was* daytime. A man didn't need starlight and darkened skies beneath which to dream.

Now, if Freud were right, then this other Norris ought to reveal in his actions the secret desires, the frustrations, of Norris' libido. By God, that would be a funny thing to see! He'd watch carefully.

There was something vastly more lifelike about this image than about the one you saw in a bedroom mirror, than the conception of yourself that resided in your mind's eye. Mirror images were as flat as photographs, while this one had depth. Norris staggered, just slightly, as he stared.

Like a dust-speck hanging stationary in air cut by a great shaft of sunlight, he felt suspended in a glassed chamber, at the other end of which shone this other Norris. Now a wind was blowing out of nowhere and carrying him, alarmed but helpless, toward the image. He was approaching it, and it was losing none of its quality of reality. He bumped against it.

"Hul-lo! It's good to see an American face. Glad you happened along."

The image was holding out its hand and taking yours and shaking it and telling you its name was Ed Blackburn. Then it led you off through a lot of narrow, smelly passages and down steep stairs to a bar room.

Struggling to bring order back to his thoughts, Norris let himself be led. The realization that this was another being, wholly separate from himself, flashed over him suddenly. He was surprised to find, at the moment of this realization, that he, Norris, was swallowing a drink of whiskey. Ed Blackburn had his face almost under Norris' nose; he was leaning over the bar and calling for a slice of lemon.

The face, Norris saw, was a perfect replica of his. Yet, considering it further, he was able to pick a dozen minor differences; probably, he thought, he'd see a good many more if his eyes weren't so bleary. It surprised him to find how intimately he knew his own face; he wondered how he had come by that certainty, for it was only infrequently that he looked in a mirror; he didn't shave himself, and when he needed a glass to set his tie right, his eyes had usually gone to the tie, not to the face about it. Blackburn, strangely, hadn't appeared to notice their resemblance.

To return to the yacht had been so distasteful to Norris that he hadn't changed his suit or shirt since morning; the pongee was wilted and wet to a crumpled bogginess. Somewhere between Maongno's bar and this one, he had accumulated a black smudge across his forehead, a smear which extended down his cheek in front of the ear. It gave him, with the rumpled, damp clothes, a frayed and grubby appearance. He didn't look at all like the son of a millionaire.

That was the reason, probably, that Blackburn said with a comradely air, "It's a rotten long pull out here, isn't it?"

"Rotten," Norris concurred. "The heat's the worst of all. A man changes out here just as a steak sweats juice over an open fire."

"Heat's stinking," Blackburn said, pushing the words out of the side of his mouth.

Norris could not avoid an interest in this man; it was as if his other self, his bodyless shadowbeing, the *Senlin* in him, had detached itself and had taken on separate life. He could not rid himself of the impression, though he consciously knew it to be absurd, that he was talking to no stranger but chatting with an intimate friend. It went further than that; he suffered the fantasy that he was talking to himself. It urged him to confidences. This must be the feeling that people have, kneeling in the dark sanctuary of the confessional. He felt impelled to discuss Night with this other self standing now beside him with a glass tilted to its mouth; he wanted to ask this other self how it was that he could admire, desire, and still look with loathing upon the same woman. He wouldn't, he felt, come to any conclusions were he to discuss it, but that only made him feel that this other couldn't be another and distinct person. And all the time he knew that this other was Ed Blackburn.

Blackburn carefully set his glass down upon the bar, placing it precisely over the damp ring which it made when he picked it up. He began to talk, twirling the glass between his fingers nervously. In a queer, oblique way he spoke about himself.

"The way I think, a man shouldn't grouse unless he's got good call to. But it's tougher than hell when you have to stick here if you hate it like I do." He wet his upper lip, outside, with his tongue, doing it very deliberately. "We-ell, it's hot here—but—you know how it is. Other places it'd be a damn sight hotter for me. Maybe too hot. Maybe we both sort of—know how that is."

Norris said, "M-mm" and Blackburn went on talking. He was, he intimated darkly, the unfortunate prey of a terrorist whose maniacal enmity he had somehow earned. The truth was that he had shot down a man on a gambling ship named the *Johanna Jones*, a corned and crapulous old scow of a vessel. And the man he had shot had had friends, two of whom had witnessed the killing.

"What I did to this laddy don't mean a thing, see? Not a thing. Just between you and me and the chairleg, it's none of his business. But that don't make the difference to him. He's still holding it in and waiting to do something to me."

"He's waiting for you to forget yourself and you're waiting for him to forget *you*."

"Something like that," Blackburn said uneasily.

He picked a cigarette from a gaudy case of red lacquer. Norris smiled when he saw Blackburn take an American banknote—a one dollar bill—from his pocket, straighten it out, tear it in half with a fatuous smirk on his face, and, after applying a match, light his cigarette with it.

A fat moon-faced Burmese was at Blackburn's side, speaking with an amazing cockney accent. He was angry, insistent, voluble. Norris was astonished at his insolence.

"Does yer 'ear me? I says I wants me money an' I wants it quick."

"You're crazy," Blackburn said coldly. "I never saw you before."

"Oho! Wot're yer givin' me?'

"Get out of here before you're thrown out. This bar is for white men. I tell you I don't know you."

The native glanced sharply at Norris, looked away, and then back again. Anger gave way to wonder on his round face, and wonder to perplexity. Suddenly this Anglicized brown man was fiercely angry again.

"Ow, there yer are. An' tryin' to cheat me. An' beggin' yer pardon," he said to Ed Blackburn, "I 'ad the wrong one. Listen, you, I wants me money now. I bin wytin' two trips fer it. You 'and it out now."

He was squarely in front of Norris by this time, his hands on his hips. Blackburn had bought some morphine from him and was now refusing to recognize the debt. He saw no reason for subduing his loud tones; drug addicts were scum to him; they had no wills and no courage. He launched upon a renewed demand, noisier and sharper than before; he climaxed this by drawing back his fist threateningly.

Norris hit him under his chin, once, viciously, and the fellow shut his mouth suddenly and collapsed. The bartender, watching with wide, scared eyes, looked at the banknote Norris laid down on the counter and nodded nervously at the command, "Don't call out."

They went up on deck and Blackburn led the way to a deserted section aft on the top deck; he seemed to know his way about the *Yorkshire Belle*.

"Thanks," he said.

Norris stood looking past the little hills, past the pagodas on top which looked like plumes in drum-major's hats, to the mountains whose plum color was grayed by distance to the dustiness of ripe grapes. They appeared desirable and unattainable. His eyes came slowly back to the swirling river below. As clean and yellow as butter, feeling its way out of the dark water near the opposite bank, was one of the long, low sandbanks so characteristic of the Irrawaddy.

"It was rather an ugly thing to do—try to palm him off on you," Blackburn began. "I'm sorry. I thought you might be taken in and pay him for me. I'm—pretty close to being broke."

"I paid him," Norris Haldorn said. "He got what he asked me for."

Some contempt edged Norris' tone, but Blackburn refused to recognize it. He continued talking in a warm, unhurried way.

"You haven't been out here long, I'll wager." It was the inevitable prelude to the cynically philosophic lecture which the white man who has lived for a while in the East delivers—or administers—to the newcomer. "The only man who knew how to get the better of this country was Buddha. You want to plant yourself under a Bo tree and look at your navel for years and years. If you try anything else, no matter what it is, to make life bearable out here, it won't work. And you'll be let down awful damned hard. The trouble is, you can't quit looking. I have done a hell of a lot of looking ..."

Norris continued staring down at the water, still strangely perturbed about Blackburn's resemblance to himself. A swarthy teak raft floated by on its long way to Poozoondoung. Was this desire to wonder about Blackburn only a subterfuge his mind was using to keep his thoughts away from Night? Ed Blackburn was talking:

"See that clump of trees there to the left of the field? There's a *dak* behind it. Best you can get out here when your funds are low. It's been my mansion lately." Neither spoke for several minutes.

As though he had found the silence uncomfortable, Blackburn began to talk rapidly again. He was almost incoherent. Norris turned suddenly and said, "Good-bye."

"Listen; can't you do something for me? I mean ——"

"No," Norris broke in, and swung away.

Ed Blackburn stood staring after him for a long time, rubbing a finger up and down the side of his face.

CHAPTER THREE

T HE cabin, large as his bedroom at home, was long and comfortable. And it was tolerably cool. Oval pipes in the ceiling, through which a refrigerant circulated, kept the heat down, and the steward took care that the sun was kept out of the cabin during the day, and that the air-conditioning machine was set going.

Norris sat on the edge of the bed, lacing his shoes. Damned idiotic, he thought, dressing for dinner in this place. Or, for that matter, dressing at all beyond a pair of linen shorts. On the river, in their heavy canoes encrusted with dry fish scales like blue scabs, and ashore in the village or in the fields, were men dressed wisely for this climate. White men or, at any rate, some classes of them, were strangely stubborn about this; they insisted on clinging to their dogma of dress and custom, no matter what the environment. Dressing here, cramming himself into a dinner coat, made him acutely uncomfortable, and yet, he admitted, he would be more uneasy if he didn't do it. There was some obscure significance in this, but he was impatient of hidden meanings. The experience itself was enough. To the devil with all else! How, for instance, could one stop to analyze the act of kissing a woman? He shuddered at the thought.

A radio message had come for him. He supposed it was from Mary Granch. It would be another of her long periodic reports, informing him of the condition of the Haldorn properties he was to take over. Mary Granch was a partner in the old line law firm that handled the Haldorn legal business. The firm kept a huge staff for the American routine work alone. Norris left the message unopened. The steward had propped it on the chiffonier, against his military brushes. As he turned to go out now, Norris stuffed the radiogram into his pocket. He'd read it later on, after dinner. If Lucia Gambier saw it she would say, he knew: "Not much longer for playing on the seas of romance, Norris dear. All play and no work, dear boy… Soon you'll be in harness with the whole world watching you."

Outside, the air pressed heavily against him. It was hot and sticky, soggy with the weight of the moisture it bore. It smelled like a Chinese bazaar, unpleasantly and sharply exotic. Across the river, agleam with floating shreds of phosphorescent wood, he saw the lanterns and torches of Paok-to, like bawdy red eyes in the dark, baleful unfocussed pupils. He wanted, desperately, to see and talk with Night, and yet, with that same duality splitting him, wanted to have done with her.

When Norris came into the dining salon, Night was staring pensively at the centerpiece, a fanlike arrangement of bright yellow flowers, heavy with fragrance. She had one hand at her hip, the long sensitive fingers directed downward along her thigh.

She looked up at Norris. Her eyes, he saw instantly, wouldn't meet his.

"Hello, fellow exile." She continued to stare at the flowers.

"Good evening. I can't see anything so absorbing in that bowl of flowers. And if you don't mind sitting down, so that I may, I'd like to begin dinner."

She sank into the chair he held for her, looked up at him over her shoulder, and suddenly smiled. At that moment he wanted to bend and kiss her. But the emotion passed, and his sudden glow of affection annoyed him. She smiled again as she spoke.

"Hungry, Norrie?"

"No; too hot," he said curtly. "I want something—anything—that will make me feel cool." Turning to go to his own place, he caught a glimpse of himself in an oblong mahogany-framed mirror that was hung on the wall. He was surprised to see how hard and grim his face looked. His lips were a thin, dark line. As he sat down he turned to look at Night again and he was a little startled by the white perfection of her shoulders. His memory swept him back to the country place where his boyhood summers had been spent. There had been a lake there and two white swans, and a black drake with a beak the color of a radish.

"Smoke?"

"Thanks, no." She rested her chin on her cupped hands, elbows on the edge of the table.

He was grateful for the illness that kept Mrs. Gambier to her cabin.

"Another of mother's usual neuralgic headaches," Night had told him languidly as she dipped her spoon into a cone of pistachio sherbet. With the spoon she dabbed and patted and sliced at the sherbet, making a pretense, meanwhile, of eating some of it. No blonde woman, as impressively slender as she was, ought to have dared wear her amethystine gown, snug-bodiced, with deep decolletage,—but Night made it seem, somehow, quite reasonable. The dress made her look more mature, less girlish.

"The mail caught up with us today ... at last." Norris glanced up sharply but there was no expression in her face to match the irony in her words.

"Why the 'at last'?"

"Oh, it does take a long time, doesn't it? Three weeks since the last letter I had from Gretchen Norman and that was only from London. It's been—why, it must be a month since we've had a New York newspaper. Oh, I meant to tell you ... Paula Waylan's married. The mail brought an announcement."

Norris took a sip of ice water before he answered. "My only reaction is mild pity for the bridegroom."

"Pity? But Paula's a gorgeous creature. Why be sorry for the man who won her?"

"Won that woman? *Won* her?" Norris laughed, flatly. "You're full of nonsense. Whoever married her, she chose him, inspected him, tested him and then deliberately and calmly reached out and took him."

"Well, I suppose you *could* call Paula's manner rather domineering and positive," Night admitted. In the same tone, a drawl, she went on, "Isn't this thing becoming too awfully fantastic, Norrie?"

"It was fantastic to start with," he replied calmly.

"Yes, but I mean coming here, to a place like Burma and just staying here without any reason. I can't believe that you're enjoying it. You don't look as if you are, I can tell you. And if you weren't here, it would be completely unbearable for me ... really dreadful." He thought he detected a thin note of mockery in the voice.

"You're perfectly free to return, you know." This was cruel. But he felt that it was necessary to provoke her. "You say the word and I'll turn the *Troubadour* around and steam for Calcutta at once—tonight, if you like. You can get a boat from there to Liverpool almost any day."

"Something's gone horribly wrong, terribly wrong with our lives, Norris." Still the drawl, still the smooth eyes somberly caressing the bowl of yellow flowers on the table. "I hate seeing all this happen, in the way it's happening. Shall I tell you how I feel about it?"

"Do." Just what, he wondered, as he watched her toy with a cube of sugar, would she reveal of the truth, of what actually stirred within her?

"I came on this trip—" She started off, evenly, bluntly.

"Oh, never mind that part of it," Norris broke in. His own ill-temper surprised him. "I'm sorry. Go ahead, Night. I didn't mean to interrupt."

"I came," she went on imperturbably, "because—call it curiosity if you like. The thing that's called the lure of adventure in the steamship travel ads, only you were the alien place to be discovered, for me. Perhaps you didn't know you'd made a reputation for yourself of being—" She hesitated, went on—"being austere. You had. And you still have. I can't destroy it. But, anyhow, I do like you. You're the first man about whom I can say that and truthfully add that I like you enough to marry you. But I don't love you."

Norris stared at her without speaking. Night looked up at him, and then began again:

"No, I don't love you; at least, in the sense that we both understand the word love. I'm attracted to you physically, right enough. I've no doubt you feel that way about me; I think that's why you've been acting as you have. But that, unfortunately, isn't love." After a moment she went on: "That's lust, and the difference is in kind, not degree. I wonder, myself, if you could care for any woman except like that. Few men can, so far as I have been able to observe. Inwardly you're fighting against that tendency. You can't decide whether to attempt my seduction or humble your pride and ask me to marry you."

"I doubt that. I think you're mistaken," Norris answered primly. "I believe in psychology," he told her stiffly, "but hardly in this raw kind of—of psycho-analysis, if that's what it is." To himself, he added that he knew what she was in love with—the Haldorn fortune. He had never heard Night speak like this; she seemed very strange, full of an aged wisdom very much in contrast with her young loveliness. Suddenly he thought he knew what she was trying to say. But the sensation flickered out the instant he stared hard into her eyes.

He listened, amazed, when his own voice said, "Yes, about my wanting you, you're right."

Night leaned back in her chair and stared at the ceiling, her chin up, so that the mellow light caressed her throat. And then she was looking into his eyes. The gesture was a challenge … or an invitation.

"I do like you—tremendously—Norris," she said. "And do give me a cigarette and relax and stop ogling."

He held his case for her, across the table. Her composure, for nineteen, was of course surprising. But she ought to be, after all, easy for him to conquer in any conflict of wills.

"I think if I'd met you under conditions that made it a sort of mutual discovery," he began easily, and faltered, lacking the phrase he wanted. He blundered on: "But this way … It's trying to make something exquisite and lovely by a mechanical, fixed process that can only make mechanical, fixed things. Making love syntheti-cally. Like the movies do it. Establishing certain conditions, put-ting two people in them, and turning the handle on the outside of the apparatus and expecting—well, something perfectly made and flawless to emerge out of the machine. If we'd met—"

"In a swimming pool, I suppose," she interrupted, "or on a desert island after a shipwreck, or in a lion's cage from which you would proceed to rescue me."

"I'm not sure that I would."

"Would what, Norrie?"

"Rescue you."

"Idiot. Of course you would. With your ideas on being noble and chivalrous, and with your concept of 'the-right-thing-to-do,' you'd brave the hungriest lion in any cage, even if the prospective rescuee happened to be fifty and very moldy of face and figure."

"That would be a problem to be faced when I reached it. We're not occupied with that. We're occupied with ... our situation, here."

"Good lord, need you be so solemn about it?"

"I'm not solemn. I'm trying to be sensible."

"Something a little more sensible would be to get out of this steam-bath country."

"It pleases me to stay here."

"A bit selfish, aren't you? And conceited? ... But, do you know, at that, I keep on having the feeling that if one would stay here long enough, something absolutely thrilling—just really terrifying—would happen?"

"That, I suppose, is what a woman would call 'her feminine intuition'. Why don't you look into your crystal globe and discover the exact particulars of this terrifying adventure you're expecting? That might be interesting."

"Oh, no. Certainly not. Just the opposite. If one knew what was going to happen, there wouldn't be any pleasure in living at all. The pleasure and the adventure—that exists in the surprise, in not knowing."

"In other words: in drifting. You'd rather do that than plan your existence. Is that it?"

"Plan it? Norrie, you're disgusting. Anybody who could be so cold-souled as to sit down and lay out a program for his life hasn't any right to be alive or to have a free will."

The full significance of that blunt sentence struck them both at once. Night was the first to speak again after a tense silence.

"Do you suppose a woman would ever take a lover if she looked into the future and planned her existence step by step?"

"Of course she would. But she might not take the one she'd first found herself attracted to. She'd pick one with ... more promise."

"Norrie, your childish conception of women's temperaments is really uncomplimentary. If we were what you seem to think we are, what an appalling lot we'd be. You should make more of a study of us. We're really quite interesting. As it is, you're ignorant."

Norris stood up. He said, "Thank you," angrily, and went out on deck.

Night watched him go. Men, she reflected, were simple, easy to understand, open. But a man was unpredictable.

Later, talking to her mother, she said, "I'll die of humiliation if I have to go back to New York and not be Mrs. Norris Haldorn. My God, the whole Junior League will be snickering. It would be dreadful."

"Unthinkable," her mother corrected.

"I couldn't bear to see anybody if that happened. Imagine the sympathy they'd try to give me, and be chuckling behind my back, the cats."

"Don't worry; you'll have him. I can see him weakening," Lucia Gambier sleepily assured her daughter through lips thick with layers of cold cream. "Go to bed, dear. When a man insults you, it shows he's excited. That's very encouraging."

"Encouragement," Night replied, "isn't very much to go to bed with."

"Wait until you have had a little more experience before you decide on that," her mother said heavily as she reached up a hand, greasy with tissue cream, to pull the chain on her bed lamp.

"Mother," Night said in the darkness, "did you ever have a lover?"

"Night! Whatever's getting into your head? There, now, go to sleep. Try not to think. Thinking puts wrinkles on your face."

❖ ❖ ❖

Feeling in his pocket for his cigarette case, Norris touched the radiogram. Mechanically he drew it out and tore it open.

It was from Richard Todd:

I'M ALL THROUGH I HAVE TO SEE YOU BEFORE I DIE THE DOCTORS GIVE ME THREE MONTHS AT MOST

DICK TODD

At once, his thoughts, like a school of minnows startled by a splash, darted in every direction. He strove to draw them together, to be calm. There seemed to be an enormous crystal globe inside his head, through which a horde of shadows floated. Richard Todd, the only lovable, the only secure and immutable thing in his world, was leaving him. His sense of loss was deep and terrible. Richard was dying. And wanted to see Norris Haldorn before he died.

A sharp hatred of life, a disgust with destiny, throbbed through him. A new fear slashed him, a premonition that he would never see Richard alive. He read the message again. It was strange that the very emotions Richard had always derided—fear, loathing, sadness—should be evoked in his dearest friend by Richard's own call.

Then, suddenly, he knew he would go back. Could he go floating foolishly about on a yacht while his friend died, wanting to see him? He wondered if Dick knew the penalty for this visit. If Dick had known, he wouldn't have sent the message, Norris decided. If Norris returned to New York unmarried, within the period set for his journeying, he forfeited the Haldorn estate—all of it—to a specified ninety-four charities for whom it would be administered by a board of trustees.

He was going to see Richard Todd. Of that he was certain. He was equally certain that he wasn't going to marry Night Gambier. He would never give her, nor her mother, that satisfaction.

What a sensation it was going to cause, he thought grimly, in the interwoven worlds in which he had moved. It would be luscious fare, too, for the newspapers. It would promptly be decided that he was demented—throwing away a fortune for friendship. And what a thundering joke it would be to return, taking Night with him, thereby violating the terms of the will, and marry her after arriving in New York. He could say to her: "I ought to tell you, darling, that I haven't a penny." Lucia Gambier would probably collapse.

Time suddenly took on an enormously enhanced value. He no longer wanted to dawdle here, but to hurry.

Across the river a giant rice tripod was silhouetted against the night sky. A fire glowed behind it. A slow steady wind had sprung up out of the north. From the bank of the swirling river a voice sang, and with it came a mournful melody from a native mandolin.

Ah-ee-a-la ah-ee-a-la

Norris wanted to get away from the yacht. He wanted to have vast, brooding trees around him, trees with their sad green leaves—things that would be at one with his grief. A sailor came at his call and took him by motor boat to the shore above the village.

Two *poun-gyees* hurried by from Paok-to on their way to the monastery with the villagers' daily offering of fish, curry, plantains and rice. Bronze jars, that gave out subdued gurgling sounds as the monks trotted, hung from their necks. Norris hadn't yet learned to differentiate between Indian faces, and the countenances of the holy beggars were curiously alike.

He thought of Ed Blackburn. An absurd plan occurred to him. Why,—in the first place, it would endanger his name. Then he remembered. His name stood for the Haldorn-Empire fortune. Your name was only what other people thought of you; take the money away and presently other people wouldn't think of you at all. Make yourself a nobody as far as wealth went, and you *would* be nobody.

Other plans, other arrangements, dissolved as he subjected them to sensible objections. This plan alone offered a bare chance of preserving what was to be his, and of permitting him, at the same time, to see Richard Todd.

He struck out in long determined strides for the *dak* Ed Blackburn had pointed out to him that afternoon from the deck of the trading steamer *Yorkshire Belle*.

He was going to offer Blackburn the chance, for whatever it was worth, to be Norris Haldorn for a while, and he was going, with an emotion almost jubilant now, to be himself a nameless being. In the darkness, he hurried forward.

CHAPTER FOUR

I T was past three o'clock when Norris rose to leave the two-room bamboo shack where he had found Blackburn. He was glad that the matter was settled. The suave manner, the sharpness of wit displayed by the other had surprised him, but they had also satisfied him that the man was capable of undertaking the weird plan with a reasonable chance of succeeding. He did not delude himself that Blackburn was an entirely reliable person; indeed, even had he believed him a thoroughly unreliable one, Norris would, he admitted, still have taken a long chance.

He classified the man facing him now as unsteady and erratic, yet, shifty as he was, possessed of certain standards.

"One thing you must remember," Norris reiterated, "is to maintain an aloof attitude toward Miss Gambier. Do you understand that? Not rude, you understand, nor discourteous, but—well, stand-offish." This objective description of his own manner he found curiously disturbing.

"You needn't worry about that," Blackburn assured him.

"But I want you to realize that that is possibly the touchiest point of all. You simply can't make a mis-step there. Your attitude toward Miss Gambier should be based on my own—duplicate it. You must like her—a great deal, in fact,—but for, er, certain reasons, you preserve a demeanor of aloofness."

"I'm a lone wolf that doesn't give a damn about any woman," Blackburn declared.

With some amusement, Norris thought of the glimpse he had had of a pair of slim brown legs in a silk skirt in the next room. A native girl. Blackburn hadn't been aware that his visitor had seen those legs. Norris was resolved, however, not to worry about this phase of the situation. He felt entirely calm now, and a little weary.

"Keep to yourself as much as possible, in your cabin, for that matter. And don't drink.'"

Blackburn nodded. "No booze."

"And one last thing, whatever it is you—you bought from that native on the steamer—whatever the stuff is, you've got to stay away from it for the time being. Your wits must be keen every second and you can't be playing with drugs."

"Oh—that," Blackburn's laugh was uneasy. "To tell you the truth, it was just feelin' low that made me do that. But now I have no need for the stuff. This chance makes me feel a damn sight better than ten bindles of it. No phoney either—that's straight.".

"I don't know whether that *is* straight or not—but if you don't keep your word, you're nine kinds of a fool."

"Keep your shirt on," Blackburn protested. "Don't think I'm a dumb boob just because you see me here. This ain't—isn't my fault; it's just the rotten way things fell for me, that's all."

He lit a cigarette. Once more Norris, watching him, was shocked at the way Blackburn unconsciously aped his own, Norris', mannerisms. This was the maddest kind of coincidence, and some day, some more tranquil day, he wanted to think about these things, wonder about them, try to reach an explanation.

Walking back to the river, he missed his way in the darkness and came to an unfinished shrine, a *htu-payon*, begun by some pious merchant whose funds had given out and who had had to abandon this monument to his piety.

It lay now, a gorgeous rubbish heap, typical of things Burman in wanton Theebaw's day. By daylight it would have appeared squalid, but now, under the hot moonlight, it was different, made glamorous by the bright silver light. There was still standing in it an image of the Gaudama, carved of teak, grotesquely atilt on its pedestal. Save for the occasional metallic chatter of a night bird, the place was quiet.

Picking his way across it, Norris came to what must have been the central chamber, only two of whose walls remained, and here he came on an old bell, tarnished, partially covered by rotting leaves. Wherever moldering leaves and dead blossoms did not cover the ruins, living vegetation, creepers and bushes and even single stalks, did their best to hurry the work of covering the stones. Norris' stick swung against the bell and it rang out in a dull, booming sound—a queer, dead kind of note. Near it, on the ground, lay another Buddha, this one of stone, the placid horror of its countenance already beginning to flatten under the erasures of heat and wind and rain. Norris sat down on the Buddha. Amusing, sitting on a god's face.

He fell asleep almost at once, as he sat there. It was already dawn when he was aroused by a hollow note from the upturned bell. He opened his eyes to see a figure standing beside him. For an instant, fluttering in that translucent world between sleep and consciousness, he was gripped by the fancy that his spirit had left his body, and was standing there gazing somberly at him. The illusion ended; he was awake.

It was Ed Blackburn. "Sorry. Too bad I was clumsy and hit the bell. You look so comfortable there on Buddha's mug."

A feeling that Blackburn had followed him, had been watching him here for a long time, seized Norris. "Thought you bedded in the *dak*."

"A touch of insomnia."

"Worried?"

Ed Blackburn laughed. "Hell, no; I'm a fatalist." He leaned against the black rim of the bell. "A man learns the dumbness of worrying his fool head about the future after he's out here a while."

Now that he was aroused, Norris had no desire to linger here. There were further preparations to be made, and he had no need to talk more with his proxy-to-be. He had already spent three hours telling Ed Blackburn what he would have to know to step confidently into the place of Norris Haldorn, had given him his cues and the mode of conduct he must pursue. Norris stood up.

"Has it occurred to you," Blackburn asked him, without moving from his easy position against the bell, "that there are more points of likeness between us than just appearance?"

"What do you mean?" Norris asked slowly. "What are you trying to say?"

"Well, just for example, the both of us coming to the same place when we were wandering around, thinking. Our minds seem to work alike. Maybe you'd like to know what's in mine."

"Not now," Norris said stiffly. "I will meet you this evening at the place agreed upon. Goodbye."

"Wait a minute." Blackburn stepped back a bit and stood in the path. "I guess we have to talk a little about money."

Norris, about to shove him aside angrily, thought better of it. After all, it wouldn't be wise to quarrel if it could be avoided.

"Money?"

"Yes. Money." The words were uttered harshly, bitterly. "You can write a check for any amount you damned well please. It's been a lot different with me. As long as we're cooperating for mutual benefit, you ought to give me a little retainer. About five thousand or so. What's it mean to you? Nothing."

Norris watched him with mounting anger. "You understand what the agreement was. Ten thousand and land you somewhere on the Pacific coast when I resume my name. You were grateful for that a little while ago."

"But not now." Norris saw he was holding a revolver. Its barrel was flecked with gold by the early-morning light. "Daddy," he said viciously, "might have to spank you. See? One shot that nobody would notice and there would be one Norris Haldorn instead of two. And that one would be me."

The pupils of his eyes, Norris saw, were strangely large; the hand holding the gun shook perceptibly.

"Anyhow, why should I be a dirty dog any longer while you play the prince? You've had your fling at the top and now somebody else has a turn coming. You be the lousy bum for a while and I'll be the gentleman and get out of this stinking hole. I won't kill you. There isn't enough justice in that. We'll just change places as you arranged, but a little ahead of time. And within a few hours the Haldorn attorneys in America will get radiograms that an insane faker is posing as me out here in Burma. They'll be warned to be on the lookout for you all right. The gall of you … pretending to be Norris Haldorn. That's a great plan. It's a lulu."

"You're mad." Norris pulled himself in for a leap, felt his loins tighten and thighs tense.

"No; just smart," Blackburn said. "I've been in a lot of rackets, but I never had anything as soft as this handed to me. I'd be a plain nut if I blew my chance now. I was kind of doubtful even after you spilled me the works, but I made a test."

Norris relaxed. "A test?"

"You were spotted here so I went out on the yacht and gave your captain some orders. He couldn't see my clothes, in the darkness. Boy, he never batted an eye. And looking into my face all the time. Hear that, guy? All the time."

Norris flung himself, trying to twist his body out of the path of a possible bullet, upon Blackburn. But there was no need for Blackburn to fire; the Gaudama achieved the same result silently. Over the upturned, outstretched hand of the statue, Norris stumbled, fell and lay still, stunned by the impact of his forehead against the ground. Very deliberately, in the manner of a man blotting his signature after putting down the pen, Ed Blackburn bent over and brought the butt of the revolver crashing against Norris' skull.

Then he turned the numb figure over, squatted down and drew a razor, an old-fashioned open-bladed razor, from his coat pocket. This he laid on the ground, and his fingers, quick and thin, slid through Norris' pockets. Some of the papers he kept, the rest he discarded, tossing them into the mouth of the old bell. Then he picked up the razor and took Norris' face under his hands. The first gash went upward from the left side of the upper lip, curving, to the sinus, slitting every muscle on the way. In the longitudinal slit on the right side of the face, he laid bare a tendon, and cut it apart. The skin, too, received his attention. And, as a final touch, he nicked a piece out of each side of the tongue, well back toward the fleshy base. That, he figured, would alter the timbre of the voice and change the enunciation entirely.

A genial expression settled on his face. He stood up now, flexed his back, and threw his coat over his shoulders. He was glad none of the blood had touched his clothes. He would wash his hands in the river.

"And that," he said to a parrot in the tree above him, "is that."

An hour later the *Troubadour* pulled into the channel and slipped downstream.

CHAPTER FIVE

THE yacht, approaching Rangoon, was rounding a great bend in the Irrawaddy. She passed *loungoes*, heavily laden with yellow paddy for the mills, bearing down the broad slow stream at a more leisurely pace than the *Troubadour*. Though it was hardly two o'clock and the land about was sunk in its mid-day sleep, a group of natives, evidently field workers, were laying fish out to dry on a bamboo platform set a little back from the bank. They looked like animated mushrooms under their enormous umbrella-shaped straw hats.

Night sat under the awning, trying to write a letter, finding the heat oppressive. Mrs. Gambier lay dozing in a deckchair.

"I don't think you had better do any sight-seeing in Rangoon, dear. We must both do as little moving as possible until we get back to a decent climate again. God knows how I bear it. First the rains and now the heat."

Night laid down her pen and stared pensively at her finger nails. "I'm still disturbed about Norris. It's beyond explanation."

"No it isn't," her mother disagreed sluggishly. "Men always do unexpected things when they're in love, darling. That change of heart Norrie had, only proved I was right about him. Night dear, do be quiet for a bit; it's a dreadful effort to have to talk."

"But I *want* to talk. You know, Norris offered to show me around Rangoon when we get there. We didn't see much coming in. But I'm sure he doesn't know any more about the place than the man in the moon, Mother. And he's so insistent about it, too.

He got very friendly and—well, I suppose you could call it vivacious. He was almost objectionable."

"I'm going to have a little talk with him—after you're married," Mrs. Gambier said. "About financial matters. He'll be glad to see that I take an interest in it. You should, too."

"Mother—I wasn't talking about that. I'm trying to tell you ————"

"But *I* was talking about that. This world isn't all cream-puffs, you know. What in the world does it matter if Norris is in a different mood today than he was yesterday, or if he is in a different mood tomorrow. You ought to be thankful for that. It won't be monotonous after you're married."

"After I'm married, after I'm married," Night mimicked irritably. "Don't you think I'm a human being? Is it so unnatural for me to show an interest in the man I—" She stopped dead.

"Of course not; it's quite right. It's nice that you *do* care about him. I'm sure I like to see you exhibiting that spirit. The proper spirit is everything. When you're as wise as I am, you'll know how much the proper spirit counts."

"Mother, what *are* you talking about?"

"Something it might do you a little good to learn," Mrs. Gambier sniffed. "Now, there's a dear, don't pout like that. You have your forehead all rolled up in wrinkles. I'm sure nothing should be troubling your sweet little head that much now."

"But I tell you he acts strange. He acts as if he's actually trying to be ingratiating. It makes me feel so queer."

"Pish and twaddle," said Mrs. Gambier, closing her eyes. "I'm going to take a nap."

Blackburn came, a bit later, searching for Night, and Lucia Gambier, drowsing, roused herself.

"Norris, I can't tell you how glad I am we are moving on away from here."

"Glad myself," Blackburn said.

In a more confidential tone, she proceeded: "I've always wanted to ask you something. Do you believe in cosmology?"

"Why—I don't know. What is it?"

"It's the—well, it's the science of—well, it's like the science of the mind and the brain and what you do with it. It's really very deep."

Blackburn, cautious, asked, "Oh, you mean casting horoscopes and stuff like that, don't you?"

"Oh, no; that's astronomy, with the stars and the moon and things. That's very good, too. No, I don't mean that. Cosmology is where you take the mind and what goes on inside it. We're all meant to be what we are and nobody can escape it. It's just planned by destiny before we're even born. Now if I were walking along the shore there and somebody would come along flying an airplane and it would fall and kill me—well, why would I get up from here and go on shore and why would that airplane come by just at that time? That's where your astronomy comes in, too. You see, it's all arranged for us."

Blackburn was uncomfortable. "Well, why do you?"

"Why do I what?"

"What you said—go ashore and get killed."

"Because—oh, it's all fated long before. It's written that it should happen that way. I just meant that as an example. Everything's the same way. The way you and Night are in love, and the way you met each other—why that's the same thing. Can't you *see* it? I think it's the loveliest, most romantic thing in the world."

"I guess there's a lot of important people who have faith in the stars, all right," Blackburn said.

"Oh, in olden times astronomy and astrology were the main things. They were the important things in all the schools in the

Middle Ages. But then they came along and put witchcraft in it and then they made them cut the whole thing out because it was spoiled with that voodoo when they began witching around."

Blackburn grinned. What luck. The woman was without guile of the sort that might expose him. "I feel like witching around a drink," he laughed. "Do you want one?"

Mrs. Gambier shook her head. "Just iced tea, I think." Coyly, she whispered: "Night is around on the other side of the deck."

They got into the *tikka gharry* a while before the violet night enwrapped the city. From a bright bronze, just above the horizon where the sun still hung, the sky faded to a light brown, clotted, at the east, with purple clouds. The city itself lay under a soft lavender mist that shaded the brilliant colors below,—the smoldering fire of the great *hte* on the Shwe Dagon, the blue-white and ochre of the great houses on Phayre Street, the ruddy tubes of the smokestacks. Night, watching, was dizzied by the splendor of it. Rangoon, now, was like the palette of a careless painter.

Blackburn vaguely sensed the delight that possessed his companion in this chaos of color before dusk. He knew Burma intimately. Rangoon and the garden of Tham-Bosam, he knew better than most whites, though without divining anything of their esoteric Eastern significance. He glowed with a sudden sense of vast power as he helped the girl from the little carriage.

His face corrugated by his most sycophantic smile, Tham-Bosam himself came to usher them into one of the little paper rooms that front on the fragrant flowering garden behind the high hedge. There, if the owner is to be believed, incessant prayers and unending propitiary offerings make the malevolent *nats* as scarce as those bodyless beings can ever be in this land.

"Thou knowest thy work?" Blackburn asked him in Burmese.

"I know, master," said Tham-Bosam gently.

"Good!"

Night stared at Blackburn, but before the question in her eyes loosed itself to move her lips, he said, "Surprised that I spoke to him in his own tongue? I've been picking up a few words on these days I've spent ashore. I'm proud of being able to order in Burmese."

The early night wind blew improvised lullabies on the wind-bells above, and the notes tinkled down like flower petals; it was pleasant in the garden of Tham-Bosam.

Around the darkening arbor the green lanterns began to glow, and the little strips of painted cloth fluttered with the mind. While Night and Blackburn tasted the best of Tham-Bosam's sesamun seeds and pungent green ginger and jasmine tea, their host was elsewhere making preparations for which he had received, an hour before, a generous gift of silver from the new master of the *Troubadour.*

The spindling native host stood by their table again. "You would be pleased to visit the principal abode of the All-Wise One?" he asked.

"You go alone," Ed Blackburn told her easily. "I've seen the Shwe Dagon before. It's worth going and I'm afraid if I go along, I'll talk about it and that's sure to spoil it for you."

Walking beside her, the squat native guide sent by Tham-Bosam said, "It is too late for you to hear all the bells, for the hour of the bell is past; but you will hear the great one."

Night was touched by a curious yearning, a desire, elusive and disturbing, as she watched the last gleaming point of the *hte* fade out. The spire paled from gold to a mauve finger, its tip lost in the twilight. At that instant the city quivered under the thundering peal of the Big Bell, quivered, and awoke for the night.

They mounted the long stairs, bathed now in lilac shadow, sunk in melancholy brooding, a brooding emphasized by the tapers lit in the lesser shrines which they passed. Norris' attitude now, his spoken preference for sitting alone in the garden while she went to the pagoda, was another abrupt shift of attitude, and one, she thought, obviously related to his earlier surliness.

Later, returning, she said aloud, "God, why can't I be free …"

The Burman took it, from the fervent, anguished tone, that she was uttering a pious ejaculation, and gazed at her with new respect. It was seldom, he believed, that beautiful women, of whatever color, were sincerely reverent, stirred by an urge at once humble and devout. Usually, in their prayers, it was neither grace nor humility nor faith they solicited, prostrate in front of the sacred image. Even here, in a place consecrated to the spirit, it was too often of the flesh that they thought. In this temple, enveloped by an invisible beneficence, an accumulation of the prayers of the faithful over ten centuries, he had overheard their whispered supplications for frivolous things.

He looked at Night with respect.

CHAPTER SIX

W ITH a pillow of wood under his head and a mat under his body, Norris watched a small moon slowly slide down the sky to sink into the jet contours of the Ko-man Hills. He trembled with pain. A month had passed, a hot Burman month, since the morning he had last seen Blackburn. He tried to collect his senses, to reconstruct the past. There seemed to be, between him and the hard surface of things, a veil; his sight and touch and hearing were dulled, and he seemed to hear the recurrent groan and crash of immense waves mounting, curling and breaking on the shores of his consciousness.

"It was written thou shouldst die, but thou wilt not, Beloved." The voice was tender, soft and solicitous, reaching him like a caress.

At the urging of the voice he slipped off again into a stupor and did not come awake until the sun was bearing high over the tawny fields and shining in upon him through the doorway. He grasped, in a vague way, that he was Norris Haldorn and that he ought not to be staying here. He ought to be about some important business, but the more he struggled to remember, the more his head pained and the heavier his distress became. Presently he ceased trying.

The girl who came in and fed him couldn't have been more than sixteen or seventeen, but that was maturity for a Burmese woman, and Narapatee was in her prime, with full breasts, and rounded thighs that became visible when she swung past in her split skirt of figured silk. She knelt beside him now, supporting his head and feeding him fruit that dripped with warm juice. He struggled to sit up. His mouth and cheeks began to burn and ache. Gently the girl restrained him. He ran his hand over his face and felt the thick ridges and lumpy cords and sunken places of the awful scars. There seemed to be a curl in his tongue. It made talking difficult.

He had, the girl informed him gravely, in a stilted English learned in the mission school, been close to death, but her love for him, together with her care, had cured him. His name was not Ed, Norris told her, and she repeated after him, "Nah-Rees", softening the word in her way. There was affectionate pity in her smile and tenderness in the way she touched his cheek. When she decided it was futile to try to help him remember that he was Ed, she found an unexpected pleasure in telling him about herself, him, who knew her so well.

Narapatee was a Saturday girl, she told him; her name, chosen after hours of consulting the stars and after long conferences between her parents, her relatives, the priests and the *lugyis*, meant Humility of the Bountiful Rains. She did not add that, notwithstanding so luscious a name and the munificence of her father in setting her up in a tiny stall in the marketplace, she had come this far, almost to the age when she would be considered undesirable, without having gotten herself a native husband. Perhaps, now that he had been changed by this sickness, Ed would not taunt her about that any more.

"Above all the rest, thou art vain and conceited," her father had berated her, chewing viciously on his cud of betel. "Hast thou not spurned the honorable offers of two most eligible and desirable and industrious young men and, by that, made thyself a woman looked on with suspicion in our village?

"And did I not," he had proceeded, growing angry as he considered his own generosity and her lack of gratitude, "at great expense and using the money from many days of toil, purchase goods for thy stall, that thou might be each day where the young men congregate and thus be enabled to show thyself before them and find a mate?

"Why art thou so undutiful?"

He became sterner, addressing her in the formal way: "Did I not, against the advice of the *lugyis*, permit you to go daily to the *dak* of the white man that you might learn his tongue, because it pleased you to learn it? Have I not permitted you to be absent from feasts and *pwes* that you might pursue this childish whim? Do you forget entirely your filial duty?"

Narapatee had listened without replying.

Had he not, her father had proceeded, lit many candles before the feet of the All-Wise One for her? "And have I not permitted you to go many nights to the white mission because you so admired the strange sleeping couches there, and liked to lie upon them in slumber? You are both ungrateful and ill-mannered. It is enough of a curse that I am sent a girl child instead of a son who might work for me. And yet, even though I do not condemn you for this, but give gifts to you and humor you, you behave like a dog."

Narapatee might have told him that her major desire had to do with departing the abode of her parents—a most depraved and unfilial yearning, to be sure, but one that she, with the easy conscience of the Burman, had reconciled completely with all the lessons she had been taught.

There must have been Kachin mountain blood in her, blood of the hard, shrewd hillmen, blood of the tribes that worked the jade veins in the high country to the east, before the English came.

A dull man, her father had said little when Narapatee had brought the white man, strangely slashed, home for nursing. The *shwe* was, he supposed, an Englishman; at least he had blonde hair. It was proper, he believed, that the sick and the maimed should be gently tended; it was in fact a grace to do it and he devoutly hoped that by the performance of this worthy work, his daughter might find new favor with the Sublime One. In the infrequent moments when he had considered the matter, her want of piety had perturbed him; in that fault, perhaps, lay a cause for her ill fortune in finding a husband.

For Norris, the girl Narapatee was the only one of the large family in the bamboo house who appeared as a definite person. The others—the squat fat oily mother and the skinny dry grandfather and the gaunt dry father and the laughing naked children with their grotesque little round swollen bellies—were strange, insubstantial beings. They were shapes having the quality, for him, of shadows through which you could move without discomfort. And the rest of the family had discovered, for their part, that the Englishman was queer, that he did not hear when you spoke, yet spoke himself when you were hidden above and no one was within his own sight to hear. It might be, they thought, that he had communion with the *nats*, and they adopted a policy of respectful indifference.

Life had become, for Norris Haldorn, a succession of days, quiet, brilliantly blue, during which he sat on the river bank in the shade of an old fig tree and let the Irrawaddy water flow peacefully past. He was content. Very often, he was full of a sudden joy that seemed to well up within him. He liked to sit with his eyes closed, feeling the broad, corky palm of the baking sun upon his skin, hearing the sultry purl and splosh of the river. He could sit like this for hours, in a warm windless nothingness, his head sunk upon his chest, his hands limp on his thighs. The villagers came to believe, after a while, that this *shwe* was a holy man, a priest and mystic of a superior kind, who turned his thoughts inward and meditated on the meaning of all things, impervious to the world outside him.

He had grown about him a translucent shell that held him safe and comfortable inside, passive and untroubled. That shell protected him in all ways. Even when the orange-colored insects with the wide wings and the vicious, painful sting, came droning and soaring about him, he lay tranquil. That was more than the natives could do. When they heard the loud, harsh buzz of the pest, they flailed their arms about their heads and ran for the shade, where the thing would not follow.

When it was blazing noon, with the sky like the inside of a glazed cobalt teacup, Norris relished the noon, and was glad. When it was early morning and the ground brewed heavy odors, he was glad that it was early morning. And for the quick dusk and the unexacting night he was grateful, too.

Sometimes curt noises troubled him; twangs, yelps, crackles, burrs—they cast a sooty fog over the clarity of his days and laid smudgy thumbs upon his memory. When the big river steamers came by, bearing hideous discords, he used to go away from the bank and walk into the dark moist woods. There he found gray and brown animals that squeaked, and birds that sang, but in these sounds there was nothing that displeased him. Other sounds he found intolerable: the river and the village sounds, especially the shriek of dry metal scraping against metal on the steamers, the creak and groan of the windlass and the hundred unnatural rumbles and stammers of a heavy vessel.

He had been sitting for hours with a smooth flat stone, laid with a smooth soft leaf, under his feet; here where the shore fell back in a shallow cove that caught the silt-filled waters and played idly with them in little eddies and whorls. He was so far below Paok-to that even the slow sounds of the lazy village in midday failed to reach him. He existed in a state of endless forepleasure, tenderly fondling beauty but never attempting the aggressive possession of it. No desire fired his pleasure; his state was suspended, placid.

Narapatee sat down beside him. A copper band that circled her ankle glittered liquidly in the sunlight. The lobes of her ears, Norris saw sleepily, held stubby cylinders of smooth clear jade. The blouse she wore was made of gauzy cloth, the same pale chrysolite shade. While the blouse made visible her golden shoulders and her breasts, it added a soft dusty film, like a shadow, upon the brightness of the brown skin.

She began to speak to him in Burmese and went on for several minutes in a plaintive tone, with her eyes on the ground. As if she felt that the subject and the occasion demanded it, she used the formal form of address.

"Why do you want me to call you by this strange name of Nah-Rees?" she asked. It came to him, unable to understand her words, that she was beseeching him to give her some sort of assurance. What it was, he did not know. "Why do you want this name when you used to like so much the pet name you taught me, Ed-Dee? What makes you so different, as if you are in a dream?" He was, she hastened to add, on the chance that there might be misunderstanding here, her adored at all times.

"At least, tell me that you know what I am saying," she implored.

Norris shrugged his shoulders.

Narapatee surrendered, as she had done before, and acquiesced to the changes in her beloved. Hardest of all to bear was his ability to converse with her only in English, for the words did not come spontaneously to her and there were so many things of love she had to say, so many intimate communications which she could say so superbly in Burmese. For these, her store of English supplied no proper equivalents.

His sickness, she decided unhappily, had robbed him of many powers. But, she consoled herself, none of his present shortcomings was willful.

Pensively she asked him, in her own tongue, "Do you remember the great jewel?" Norris stared at her uncomprehendingly. "The jewel, the eye of fire, of Buddha!" she exclaimed. Then she remembered and asked him in English.

"The jewel of the small temple, Nah-Rees? You recall it? We—together—found—it … we."

"Jewel? No," Norris said stolidly.

Narapatee took his hand between hers. "Tomorrow we shall look upon it again. We go tomorrow to the little temple. So." She pointed to the north, where strings of blue smoke hung over a thin row of palms on the far edge of the rice fields. "There we go. Up and beyond and up."

"There we go," Norris echoed, "There."

Down into the river with their mahouts came two elephants. Easing their bulks, like massive chunks of gray dough, into the tepid yellow water, they uttered vast snorts of satisfaction while the emaciated drivers climbed over them like insects, currying them with heavy metal rakes. This toilet was accompanied by slobbering and slushing sounds. Every few seconds one of the beasts would thrust his trunk up and from the stiffened nozzle would jet a narrow stream of dirty water that curved up gracefully before it broke into a fine spray which caught the sunlight and made momentary brilliant rainbows.

Finally the drivers were done. They sat down on the bank and ate their fish and rice and seeds while one of the elephants lay on his side in the water and the other cropped tender green shoots on the brink. Neither elephant nor man would toil in the fields at midday. Norris turned on his back and let his eyes wander across the sky.

A little naked boy, with huge grave eyes and a pendulous belly hanging over pipestem legs, came up. His thin hand held a dead grub or a slug of some soft, fat sort. Standing there, he put the yellowish-creamy thing into his mouth and began to chew it. Narapatee shrilled angrily at him. The boy looked up at her in hurt surprise, and when she jumped up, crying she would take the foul thing from his mouth, he ran off furiously. The girl came back after a few futile steps in pursuit, and sat down again beside Norris.

Suddenly Norris found himself talking, his mind reacting to the stimulus of the child's actions. "That is what love may be. It can be terrible, like that slug the little boy held, Narapatee; it can be full of foul matter, yellow and swollen. And then it dies quickly."

"Faugh!" She screwed her face into a grimace and shook her head. "What words are these, *Shwe?* That you say love is like a filthy slug? Love is of the red flowers, of the red flowers and the deep green woods, and of soft words softly spoken. It burns as the *htes* on the temples, *Shwe. Aiya*, you are strange, beloved." She sighed before she continued, "The ways of men are strange but their words are stranger. Often I do not understand you; your words have no meaning. Since I love you, you must not change any more. You must stay."

"I will stay," Norris said.

"You will not go away?"

"Go away?" Norris looked across the river and then back at the girl. "There is neither going nor coming, nor words of change. Here I am and here I stay."

But Narapatee whispered, "You are not the same as he who was with me before. No. You are another." Her hands touched his face and flew back to her own lips in concern. Perplexity creased her forehead. "Yet you are the same. The two must be one." She nodded. "The two must be one ..."

The days sailed by like languid yellow birds. One morning Norris stood by the ladder that led up to the porch of the bamboo house, smoking a cheroot the size and color of a fat candle. From the house there came a curious medley, made up of the wild shrieking of a child in frenzy and pain, and the wail and throb of Burman music, with an overtone of lusty laughter. Inside, he knew, they were piercing the ear's of Narapatee's sister, who was a Wednesday girl. They were holding her flat upon a mat while the women forced the wire through the soft brown lobes. The music was to drive the *nats* away, perhaps to fool them into believing this was some ordinary festival. So long as the *nats* did not hear the child's cries, she was safe from their malignant influence.

Norris walked south to where a great sandbar, curving back to the shore, formed a quiet bayou. Standing on its edge, he saw a watersnake whip itself across the surface of the thick water, its head stiffly erect and its black tongue flickering. Its speed increased until it was a sinuous gray-blue thread curling over the brown disc of the river. The snake was headed for the sandbar where a thousand flies had clustered, like a glaucous blue-black sponge, upon the body of a bird. Going on, Norris came to the road that led to the home of a wealthy man. In a pool within the garden, where white lotus flowers shone from their smooth platters of green, another snake flung itself out of the water and onto the hot flagging. This one, Norris saw, was a cobra, a small one, and it was uncomfortable on the stones. Instead of settling down, it kept its head raised, and its tail continued to squirm. Norris picked up a heavy stone and moved slowly toward the reptile.

The snake watched him. Its hood swelled. Its coils drew in. With a flip of his hand, Norris threw the stone into the pool behind the snake. It turned and hurled itself in one incredible movement, falling with a mad hissing into the water. When it emerged this time, Norris caught it behind the neck with a pronged stick and held it while he pounded it to death.

Then he sat down and looked contentedly into the still purple pond until it was noon, when he went back to the bamboo house to eat rice out of the family pot and curry out of the little saucer Narapatee had given him. He told her proudly about the snake and she relayed the news to the family who stopped their frantic dipping and scooping and gulping long enough to emit cries of approbation.

When he had eaten his fill, Narapatee's father wiped his lips upon the back of his skinny wrist and leaned forward. "When dost thou wed the white man, daughter?"

The blunt question irritated the girl and, because it was asked before the other members of the family, humiliated her. "When I please," she answered sharply. Women enjoyed a freedom in Burma which they enjoyed nowhere else in India.

The father patted his bulging stomach thoughtfully for a time and then reached to the tray and took a fiery betel cud which he tucked between his jaws. He sat chewing, getting his mouth juices flowing, before he spoke again.

"Another moon and no more he stays under this roof without laboring, daughter. Beyond that he shall not eat the fruits of our toil while he sits and dreams by the river through the day."

There was in his tone now a dignity it had not owned before, a force that moved Narapatee to bow her head and say, "I hear thee." Something, she realized, had to be done at once. She felt, tucked in her skirt, a coin, the proceeds of a sale of cloth the day before. It would pay a boatman to ferry them across the river and to bring them back later. She called to Norris. He rose, satisfied to let her will control him, and followed her out onto the narrow veranda and down the rickety ladder to the ground.

Between the fiery sky and the fiery earth, there was but one cool place in Burma, a hazy smudge of green to the north. It was here they were going, the girl told him when they stepped from the boat. They were going to a pagoda far off in the hills. Its *kyaung-taga*, she added, as they walked, must have been very wise to have built it where it was, because only the very pious would go so far to worship in so small a shrine and thus the superior piety of the supplicants would continuously attest the wisdom and devotion of the builder.

It took them two hours to reach the beginning of the hill country, cutting their way across the muddy rice fields. It might have been two days or two minutes … time had ceased to have meaning for Norris. They climbed steadily. After passing the neat terraced gardens of a monastery, they came presently to the deeper bowers of trees. No path appeared open before them, but when they reached the fringe of the forest and plunged in, they saw lanes running in every direction. The trees dripped with moisture and were lit by a kind of milky sunlight, except in the infrequent open spaces where the light was clear golden. Occasionally the musteloid of a teak trunk showed, but this was not wild country and most of the really heavy teak had been cleared by the companies and hauled away by elephants.

Occasionally a bird would cry with what seemed unnecessary stridency. Twice, parrots swished across in front of their faces, big parrots with wings of bright jasper, underfeathers of cerise and tails of topaz. Except for this, it was wonderfully quiet. Norris was very happy; a glow of gladness seemed to be pouring into him from every shining leaf, brimming from the wine-red bell-shaped flowers that grew about the trunks of trees. It was the kind of ecstasy that left him calm, certain in the knowledge that it could never end, that its source was inexhaustible. It was a strange sort of bliss because it had no beginning and no object, it depended on nothing and yet was connected, somehow, with everything.

The way led down now, and they came to a torpid little stream, russet colored. Fording it, Narapatee bent down, scooped a handful of inky pebbles, and tossed them up in the air in an excess of naive glee. Like a shower of polished jet beads, they rained down on the slow stream.

"The day is good," she said, holding her face up to the sky. Norris nodded. Yes, it was very good. She had described it well. When you had said this was very good, there was nothing more to be said; that expressed everything. He had no desire to talk. They walked on into the thicker, darker depths where steam, sucked from the ground, heavy with the aromatic odors of the soil and the leaves, lay low and heavy in the air.

Only once did the old numbing pain trouble him, the pain of trying to think of some faraway and forgotten time when there had been something he had had to do which he had not done. He shook his head and let the futile worry slide away and the joy returned, unclouded.

It was almost dusk when they mounted the last steep hill and stood before the little temple. In front of it, and so tiny that it could reflect only a portion of the pagoda, lay a pool, square and deep, its surface, like onyx, unmarred by any floating flower. Narapatee stopped as she stood over it and her face was mirrored for an instant in its smooth surface. They went inside the pagoda. Here the girl left him while she lit two lanterns, one of crimson and the other of blue-green, which she hung over the gilded balustrade. Behind this, there reclined with placid, smiling face, head propped on one hand, a huge wooden image of the Gaudama. Under the diffused light of the lanterns, the face of the idol shone a sullen red and the body a ghastly blue.

Neither for resting nor for prayer had they come, Narapatee told him, holding her hand in his, tightly. Then, with a lack of reverence that would have shocked her father, the girl climbed nimbly over the railing and squirmed upon the great torso of the statue, gorgeous in garments of lacquered wood.

Straddling the middle of the Gaudama, she pulled herself toward its head until, leaning forward, she could touch the flat, elongated lobe of the left ear that drooped to the shoulder. She seized it and tugged violently, and the lobe parted from the ear. Narapatee was now under the red glow and it added a rich tone to her skin, as if she were laved by some phosphorescent oil. Norris, at her beckoning, jumped over the rail, climbed up beside her on the Buddha's shoulder, and looked to where she pointed, at an orifice at the bottom of the ear, exposed by the moving of the lobe.

Her eyes glistened in the colored light.

"Do you not remember?"

Norris shook his head gravely; it made him sad that he was not entirely as she wished. "No; I have not been here before."

Narapatee sighed and touched a tremulous hand to his scarred face. Then she reached into the ear of the god and when she withdrew her hand it held a monstrous ruby. Above this, and fastened to it by claws of gold, burned a diamond, somewhat smaller. The ruby must have weighed a hundred carats; it shone like claret held to sunlight. The diamond, perhaps seventy carats, was imperfect; a faint tinge of saffron marred it. The girl held both jewels, hooked by the gold strands, up to the colored light. The diamond burned fiercely with its own fire, but the ruby absorbed the weird red rays from above.

The fury that was the brilliance of the stones fascinated Norris. Never, he thought, had he seen anything so strange or so wonderful. He had no desire to touch or fondle the gems. Narapatee held them up in front of her face and Norris looked into her eyes. The heavy lashes engaged him. He examined them carefully. Suddenly Narapatee turned her eyes full on him. His entire being seemed to be vibrating. Confusion left him glowing inwardly as he breathlessly watched the shifting outlines of her body. Narapatee had moved from the idol and was standing on the ground. Her eyes scarcely reached the peak of the wooden shoulder.

"You are to have this jewel. I give it to you again. But it cannot leave here until we are wed."

"No," Norris said, dazed. He leaned forward and kissed the brown girl. The stirrings of a disturbed memory subsided, lost in the heady uproar of emotions.

CHAPTER SEVEN

NARAPATEE'S father was perturbed and elated over the match. It flattered his pride that a white *shwe* was to be formally inducted into his family. But it troubled him that he would probably have to support his daughter's curious husband.

Meanwhile, relatives proceeded with plans for the wedding. Burmese weddings were usually simple, because the Burmese could not afford the Western adornments. After the rites it was customary for husband and wife to slip away together into the forest, not to reappear again for a fortnight or so during which time they enjoyed a privacy complete and beautiful.

Her marriage, Narapatee had however decided, was to be a sumptuous affair which would be climaxed by a magnificent banquet for all her relatives. On her fingers, she recited items of the menu: tamarinds and rice and seeds and curry, fish and ginger, strong chili, and many other delectable dishes.

While these preparations were going forward, to the accompaniment of shrill conversation and strident-toned commands, Norris continued his passive and tranquil existence.

He walked along the river bank with his head up, staring squarely at the sun. He would stare like this for a minute and then drop his eyes to rest them. He liked the savage light and the heat. He strained to it eagerly.

Out on the river, a wide-beamed old steamer, heavily-loaded, was beginning to veer over toward the village. When the sharp boat sounds became disturbing, Norris turned and walked away from the water. He selected a narrow path and for an hour he followed it slowly, unseeingly.

Before him, now, lay a great upturned, tarnished bell and close to it, on the ground, a fallen image. The bell attracted his attention; it stirred congealed memories deep within him. Suddenly he turned and angrily kicked a stone so that it hit the bell. A protesting, booming groan came from the bell. The sound made him sway dizzily; he sat stiffly down on the metal rim. Varicolored spheres whirled around him. He felt weak; his head drooped forward heavily. The sudden jerk of his neck as his head fell forward cleared his mind. He stood up angrily. He wanted to walk; nothing was going to make him sit down. His head ached furiously. The whirling increased; the green bushes, the trees, the creepers of the *htu-payon* flew and swirled about him in sickening, silent convolutions. So much movement without any sound—that was what frightened him. Unable to withstand the nausea any longer, he opened his eyes. The mad gyrations of the foliage flung him to the ground. A parade of faces moved slowly before him. The faces merged, dissolved, reformed again. He saw that the faces were replicas of his own. And yet they were not his own. The absence of sound was complete, oppressive and awesome.

The whirling slowly stopped; the faces continued to form and reform. Suddenly all the faces merged and became one face.

He knew, abruptly, that it was the face of Ed Blackburn. He remembered. Remembered—good God! was Richard Todd dead?—what he had to do. Remembered Night Gambier. How long had he been here? He remembered Narapatee and the days and nights beside the Irrawaddy. How many days must have slid by, he could not guess. And he remembered the jewel of the little temple, and his approaching marriage.

He crawled to his knees and sat back on his haunches. The picture of Blackburn holding a revolver that glinted in the early sun was painfully clear in his mind. The pain his torn, scarred face had caused him—that, too, was clear. And all of what Blackburn had planned became apparent.

Norris began searching the ground. Inside the chalice of the bell, where Blackburn had tossed them, he found some of the papers. There was no passport, no letters, no identification cards. There was, however, the radio message from Richard Todd, and a book of travelers' checks. Blackburn had discarded the checks because of Norris' signature. There was about ten thousand dollars, Norris saw. He went through the checks again to be certain; there were just nine thousand and eight hundred dollars. That, he reflected grimly, was all that remained to Norris Haldorn. That, and a thick, ragged beard and a dark brown skin. And a native girl.

He knew at once what he was going to do. Of course. There was only one thing he could do. Then he realized it would hurt Narapatee and he was sad about going. For a moment he was ashamed of his weakness. After all, she was only a nigger, even though he had loved her. But he could not help feeling sorry.

Money. He would have to have a supply of it; the thought dismayed him. Though he now possessed the travelers' checks, there would unquestionably be some difficulty in cashing them. A plan occurred to him. Its conception and growth was so strange and so sudden; it resembled the behavior of those little green and purple paper pellets the Japanese manufactured which, on being immersed in a bowl of water, suddenly and gorgeously unfolded into fantastic flowers, into trees and kites, into dragons and flags and faces.

From a monk, Norris inquired the road to Meterdate's place. It lay on a straight line from the river, otherwise it was more than likely the directions would have been worthless.

The thick, moist perfume of plant flesh and wet soil and flowers struck his senses with peculiar power, and he was reminded that, seductive as the odor was, it yet touched on the putrid and the fetid. It was both sweet and evil.

He might not, it occurred to him, be able to convince Meterdate of his identity without some unusually persuasive arguments.

Sometimes, peering up through the interwoven foliage, he saw mysterious green lights, like the wide green tongues of huge tropic monsters, made by the sunlight as it was mirrored and remirrored on the surface of the bright leaves.

A soaring purpose, a wild zeal raised him up, exalted him and set him trembling with an unaccountable sensation of triumphant struggle. He was a man alone, a pilgrim moving dauntlessly along a road beset with horrors, to a high shrine shining far above; and the promise of peril and the prospect of strife thrilled him more than the assurance of a future peace. It was to this, after all, that he was dedicated. His father, a buoyant voice within him counseled, had also fought alone. He was, like the prophet Ezekiel, a man who had been a captive, seeing visions terrible and wonderful.

He exulted, as he moved along, in his physical strength. A mango tree stretched a stiff, weighted branch over the path. Impulsively, Norris snatched and broke it away from the trunk.

As he proceeded toward Meterdate's place his thoughts quieted. He wondered, now, if it wouldn't be possible to do something about this strange, fuzzy enunciation his mutilated tongue imposed. Perhaps. But his hands, running over his face, told him he mustn't have hope there.

The soil was changing, becoming darker. Presently it turned black. There—that must be it. On the side of a low hill, placed for protection and picturesqueness, was a typical English tropical bungalow, set up on the familiar stilts. Unlike white men's places in Rangoon, it had doors instead of cloth hangings—and, wonder of wonders, it had windows.

The house seemed untenanted; Norris noticed this apprehensively. It was silent and unkempt. Some of the windows were curtained. The paint was growing streaky. That wasn't like a planter. Painting was necessary at least twice a year if a house was to be protected from the corroding climate and from the termites.

As Norris approached, his apprehension mounted. The garden had gone lush and wild.

Well, it had to be Meterdate or no one. There was no other white man in the region who had known him; even had there been anyone else it was entirely improbable that he would believe the story Norris would have to tell, particularly since his appearance had changed so much.

Norris tapped with the knocker on the door. Then, anxiously, he rapped loudly with his knuckles while he called aloud.

After an interval of perhaps two or three minutes he heard the sound of someone moving inside the house. Norris looked up at the uncurtained window at the left of the door. There, back to back, two heads on two necks eyed him over two thin shoulders. He stood still for an instant without speaking. The coiffure, the faces, were identical and he was reminded of the head of a queen of clubs in a deck of playing cards.

The heads disappeared; a moment later the door swung open. Two women stood there in the doorway, two women who were one. They were joined together along their spines by a bridge of flesh and bone, high up, not far below the shoulder blades.

"Mr. Meterdate—is he in, please?" Norris said finally. He spoke in English.

"Nobody can see," one of the women said. They were both small, probably not more than five feet and three inches tall.

"Yes, I know. I understand," Norris said, "but this is tremendously important. A life and death matter. Must see *shwe*. Quick."

Suddenly Norris remembered Meterdate's references to his housekeepers. These must be they. Their attitude was openly hostile.

"Nobody see big boss," the same woman said again. "Nobody," the other one echoed. The faces of both were hard and small, rather gnomelike.

"I must see him. Where is he?"

"He sick. Nobody can see."

Norris understood in that moment what it was that contributed to the air of unreality, of eeriness about Meterdate's house. This was a plantation. There should have been native boys about, laborers and house servants. There weren't.

Two little yoked women staring crabwise at him. Whether they were Malayan or Siamese or some uncommon mixture of brown and yellow and white blood, he couldn't decide. There they stood, silent, suspicious.

Norris gestured impatiently. He meant, in a moment, to push his way into the house. That gesture was unfortunate. The housekeepers jumped back like frightened lizards and slammed the door.

Norris shouted for Meterdate. He tried to force the door. He heard windows being hastily closed.

There wasn't any one to whom he could go for official aid, and he had no mind to get native help. He had to keep clear of the natives, with Narapatee in mind. And he had to act quickly.

The porch ran around three sides of the bungalow. There were several other, doors, all heavy, all locked. Unusual, to find doors like that here. It was quite possible that a bullet would meet him if the minds of the housekeepers were as unorthodox as their appearance and conduct thus far had indicated. But he had to get in. He was convinced the planter was inside.

Strained, and as if in the far distance, Meterdate's voice was audible from inside the house. Or was it imagination? Norris couldn't say. If it *were* the planter, then the words were as if spoken in an ordinary tone, as to volume, but of a strained and unnatural timbre and pitch.

A lath lay on the railing of the porch and, standing to one side, Norris smashed a window. He ran swiftly around to a window on the opposite side, crashed it, and crawled into the house, tearing his shoulder on a jagged splinter of glass.

The house was baking hot inside, oppressive with static, ovenlike heat. Norris made his way cautiously through the rooms. Again the necessity for speed whipped him inwardly. His world was upside down and had to be righted.

Approaching a bedroom in the rear of the house he moved more stealthily. Behind that door, he thought, a voice spoke. He went past the closed door, pressed himself back against the wall, stretched out his hand and silently opened the door. Bending, he leaned forward and peered in.

Meterdate lay there on a high oblong table. He was naked from the waist up; below, he wore a pair of rumpled white linen trousers. And in the first glance Norris saw that the man was paralyzed.

Only in his face did life show. His body lay in that peculiar limp slackness that betokened dead nerves and dead muscles. His face held an expression of awful suffering and it was suffused with a terrifying dark red color. His eyes stared fixedly at the ceiling. His lips were tightly compressed; his forehead furrowed.

Beside the table sat the spectral housekeepers, a thin soapy sweat on their faces, lost in a sort of trance, rapt and stiff.

A fly, bloated and black, settled on Meterdate's face. It rubbed its front legs together unctuously and crawled slowly down just under the rim of his eye. This must have cost the man great torment, judging from the contortions of his face, but he was powerless to brush the fly away.

The housekeepers sat immobile on their stools, eyes closed.

Norris Haldorn began to understand what had happened. He recalled Meterdate's jeering references to the women's concern with spirits. In women like these, set apart from others by physical deformity, such an interest was likely to become morbid, all-possessing. With Bruce Meterdate stricken with apoplexy, they had quite naturally resorted to those same phantoms to help him. What was going on in the room now was probably some manifestation of the women's belief. And the disappearance of the natives was no longer inexplicable. On any malformed person they looked with superstitious awe; on two such as these, they would look with absolute terror. Let the housekeepers threaten them, order them away, and five minutes would be ample for the disappearance of every native attached to the planter's service.

Meterdate's mouth opened wide—apparently he had to stretch his throat in order to help his larynx function—and he spoke. Plainly, he was trying to shout. But the words issued in what was hardly more than a hoarse whisper; they reached Norris a strained murmur. The wonder was that the affliction permitted him to breathe, that it hadn't robbed his diaphragm and rib muscles of their strength. As it was, his respiration amounted to no more than the faintest swelling and contraction. The skin of his face shone as if it had been covered with oil.

"Go get a doctor," was what he said. "Get me a white man—anybody. Please ... please. Benda, Kilto, listen to me ..."

The women didn't move.

"I tell you I heard somebody," Meterdate persisted. "Tell them to come in here and help—and help me. Do what I tell you." His voice faded. "You bloody torturers."

A shuddering sigh trembled from one of the women; the other, an instant later, echoed it. They had, Norris saw, to breathe that way, in cycles; had they inhaled or exhaled in unison it must have caused acute discomfort to them, joined as they were.

As Norris watched, speculating on how best to dispose of the women and yet avoid any chance of their harming the helpless Meterdate, they rose and, twitching as with locomotor ataxia, put their dirty hands on the table. One of them moaned. The table rocked gently and settled back. It jiggled, and Meterdate's body shook and wobbled like congealed jelly.

Norris bent low and came through the door. Touching the orgasm of their rites, the house-keepers suddenly collapsed. They slid awkwardly to the floor and lay there, very still, breathing noisily, as if their throats were full of phlegm.

Beside the table now, Norris put his hand on Meterdate's forehead.

"Meterdate," he said. "Take it easy, old man."

The man's eyes expressed relief his body could not. "Oh, blessed God," he moaned.

"Hang on and I'll have you out of this in a jiffy."

"God, what those beasts have done to me. Who are you?"

"Never mind. Leave the questions until later and save your strength. You'll need it because I have to get you out of here."

With difficulty, Norris dragged the still insensible house-keepers into another room and locked the door. Though the window in it was one of those he had smashed, there was no danger of the women going through it: their physical handicap would make that impossible.

He took water and bathed Meterdate's face. He also brought the sick planter a drink of whiskey from a bottle he found in the living room.

"I don't know who you are, but if you'll stick by me you won't be sorry," Meterdate managed to say. "Don't go away, for God's sake."

"You *do* know who I am but you don't recognize me," Norris replied. "Don't bother your head about it now. I'll explain later."

Meterdate had to talk. And after a few sentences he grew more quiet, his words less excited. "This filthy thing grabbed me a week ago—no, six days—I can't be sure—can't remember. Knocked me over. Those devils took their chance to get back at me for tweaking them. All they had to do was look hard at them and every last one of my boys went bingo—scared silly. Ever since, they've been at it like this." Again he was excited. "They talk to ghosts. They're mad. I'll die … I'll die. Get me out of this."

"I'll get you out. You've had a rough time but you'll come out straight now."

"Quick—get yourself some clothes. In the closet in the next room. No! No! Wait! Don't leave me alone. Don't leave me alone again."

"No need to. There's duds right here in the room. Are you in any pain?"

"No. God, I wish I were. If I could only know I had a body left. I feel as if my neck were tacked onto a big lump of cold lead. It's rotten, I tell you. I don't believe in God. To hell with God! Why am I hit like this? How could there be a good God who could invent a thing like this that's got me? There's no——"

"Hold on, Meterdate; take a grip on yourself. Don't get hysterical. We've got to think about practical things. You're going to pull out of this all right. Tell me, have you got any kind of a conveyance around here?"

"Yes; a Ford, up the hill about fifty yards. It will be there. The natives would never touch it. They're scared to death of it. Get me down to a government hospital and you'll never regret it. Don't leave me. You won't leave me, will you?"

"Not for wild horses. Where will I find the fuel for the car? We've got to hurry."

"Fuel? God, what's happened to me? Yes, the fuel. It's in the steel shed behind the house. The keys to the padlock are in my pants pocket. I can't feel them but they must be there."

"Yes. Here's the ring. Which key?"

"The stubby one. It's got an S scratched on it. Got it?"

"Yes."

"Now then, man, wait a minute. For Christ's sake, don't leave me alone before you tie up those two devils."

"You needn't worry. They're locked up."

The soothing effect of this on Meterdate was remarkable. He was almost composed. "Now, listen. In the right rear corner of the shed you'll find a small safe. It will be there. Nobody could get into that shed. I designed it myself. It's steel all around and concrete flooring, lined with metal. The safe is sitting right there.... Give me another drop, will you? It helps my head. Thanks. I want you to open that safe and take what's in it along with us. I'm trusting you. I don't know who you are but you wouldn't have helped me if you weren't all right."

"Meterdate," Norris said gently, "do you remember having a conversation about Huxley? And about Conan Doyle and Sir Oliver Lodge? Do you remember? We were both a little drunk."

He held himself in front of Meterdate's immovable head. "Remember?"

"Yes," the planter breathed finally. "Yes; I remember. You're not Haldorn. It doesn't matter. You're a white man. I trust you. Look, the combination of that safe is twelve left, nine right, ten left, eleven left and then straight around to one right and open. Got it?"

"Twelve left, nine right, ten left, eleven left, one right. Yes. Hold tight. I'll be right back."

Norris stood on the deck of the river steamer. Clouds of fireflies pricked the thick darkness like bright needles. Far and mournful came the howls of lean wild dogs. That patiently resigned and unhappy sound, the complaining creak of bullock carts, came occasionally across the water.

A doctor was fortunately aboard ship; a weary man with a sad smile, bound for home on a furlough. He was now in Bruce Meterdate's cabin. The planter had seemed a little improved today. But it had become plain that the best that could be expected for him was a few years of helpless imprisonment in bed. Perhaps—the doctor had been cautious—the recovery of sensation in an arm might be hoped for. But no more than that.

To transport Meterdate a foot farther than necessary would be brutal; that was obvious. The hospital in Rangoon would certainly be the end of the trail for him. But at least a good many things to make him comfortable, to divert his mind, could be done there.

Meterdate hadn't a relative, here or home in England. That, at any rate, was what he told Norris. He may have had relatives at home, but preferred not to see them. It was often true of men who stayed here permanently that they cut themselves off utterly from any home ties.

Across the water came the throat-clutching, stomach-turning odor of the great bales of unsalted rotting fish, the stuff the Burmese had, as white men had bread.

The doctor came down the deck, bearing the clean smell of lysol and, faintly, the greasy smell of burned wax.

"You'd better come," he said to Norris.

Meterdate was dying, Norris saw. His still hands, outside the sheet, were blue under their horehound tan.

In a terrible cold whisper he said: "All there is left of me is a … a head. I'm nothing but a head. Got a sack of lead tied to it. Nothing but bloody lead dangling down." He moved into further reaches of delirium. "A head ought to have a *gaung-baung* on it. Not proper for a gentleman in Burma to go round without his *gaung-baung*. I want a blue one. Nobody else got a blue one … ever had a blue one … all pink ones." He stopped. His mouth remained open.

"That's all," the doctor said formally. "He's gone."

Norris buried Bruce Meterdate in the English cemetery.

Since Meterdate had died aboard ship, the captain of the steamer, together with the physician, made the reports to the authorities. Norris considered his duty done when he had informed the captain about Meterdate's plantation, that title to it might move through the proper probate channels.

And he had found by discreet inquiries that it was true that the planter had had no known relatives to inherit from him.

It had not been necessary to carry through what he had planned. He had meant to try to induce Meterdate to loan him the value of the travelers' checks, taking them as security.

But Meterdate was gone—and Norris had the cash he had taken, on the former's directions, from the safe in the steel shed. Good Bank of England notes, the total pretty close to the full amount of the travelers' checks. Curious that the planter had kept that much cash by him. It had, at that, been secure. Lacking an explosive, no one could have entered that shed. And, inside, a burglar would still have had the problem of opening that remarkably strong little safe.

Norris intended, when he was again in a position to do so, to send the money back here and have it credited to the planter's estate. It would, of course, revert to the government. But the debt would be satisfied. Meantime, as he saw it, no one was going to suffer by his using that cash.

He was sorry he had not been empowered to go sooner to Meterdate's place. He wondered if some one had come to release the housekeepers. And he couldn't say that, if no one had, he particularly cared, now.

At Rangoon he prowled the incredibly odorous miles of quays until he found a listing, stinking tramp steamer whose master agreed to carry him as supercargo up through the China Sea and then, after loading at Shanghai, across the Pacific to San Francisco. Norris had to give him two thousand dollars before the captain let him set a foot on the ship.

And when they were halfway across, the captain said he had changed his mind. He was afraid of the plan, he told Norris, spitting to hide his embarrassment at having to make such an admission. In the end it was necessary for Norris to agree to a modified plan of landing at a cove in Tomales Bay from which point he would have to make his way over the coastal hills and down to Sausalito and so to San Francisco. From there he would entrain for New York, and Richard Todd. To cable, he had decided, would be dangerous. What Blackburn had been up to he could not guess. At least, Norris thought ruefully, he ran little chance of being recognized. He was disguised superbly; and the disguise was one he couldn't shed.

The way over the unbelievably dreary plateau from Bolinas, on the bleak sea point, to Sausalito, on the bay, was no easy trudge for a man unacquainted with the region and without provisions of any sort.

Norris, deposited on the beach, had a suitcase full of clothes in his hand and a pistol in a holster under his arm. Somewhere along the route he dropped the suitcase. He kept cutting over the open country because the road, two feet deep under sandy dust, made walking almost impossible. And when he shuffled off the ferry that brought him from Sausalito to San Francisco, and stumbled out onto Hyde Street, his vast weariness overcame him and made him ill. Of the next day and the following night there was little he was able later to recall.

He awoke in a third-rate lodging house, on Turk Street, in a room full of the smell of cooking cabbage and the smell of dusty wood and dusty curtains. He felt weak and nauseated. There was a long scratch on the back of his hand. His hat and coat were on the floor. His watch was missing. The holster, empty, was still strapped around his chest, but he still had his money.

That night he left for New York.

Meanwhile, up the River Irrawaddy in the village of Paok-to, Narapatee shouted angrily at her bald, old uncle. He squatted on his raveled mat without speaking until she was quite finished. He possessed but one eye, having lost the other as a child, but the good orb had witnessed much.

"I have read," he answered her, reaching for a new cud of betel from the brass pot, "of maidens who have pursued their betrothed in the might and the right of the wedding promise, and saved them from those that meant harm. However, the wise men, daughter, would have thee accept thy fate without complaint. This life is brief. Therefore, compose thyself and stifle thy passion. Thou must pursue thy lover with earnest prayers."

She smothered an impulse to pour out to him her plans. The money was sewed in the hem of her single-hitch skirt, and she was of no mind to compose herself and pray. Her uncle closed his one eye and chewed his betel methodically. Narapatee stared at him in disgust. The interview, obviously, was over.

If the Sabwaw of Hsipaw had picked Narapatee to join the company of those that graced his concubinage and had subsequently changed his mind, there would have been nothing for her to do save passively to bemoan her fate. But the *Shwe* Haldorn was different; a foreigner, a white man. He was, she believed, an Englishman. All white men, so far as she knew, were English. She had pictured with rapture the days ahead. She pictured them, now, with determination.

The sky shone pale amber and red at sunset, but slender Narapatee had thought for none of it. She departed the soggy roof of her fathers, prepared to be fanatically vengeful or meltingly tender to the man she sought. She had almost two pounds in money and she had the diamond and ruby jewel of the little pagoda. With them she felt prepared....

On the ninth day after she came to the harbor, Narapatee met a young Malay whom she had followed from a pier. He was a sailor, and if one desired to go on the sea, one had to go to sailors. This one had a sly, narrow face and a hare-lip. He was a member of the crew of the schooner *Bondago*, and she sailed, he told her earnestly after learning she wanted to go there, to England.

"My ship go to England, Liverpool," he said blandly as he crossed his yellow arms over his yellow chest.

"England," Narapatee breathed. She nodded. "To England."

"All very easy," he assured her. "I can do everything. Come here tomorrow." But tomorrow was too long to wait for what he saw in front of him, so he spoke, that afternoon, to the master of the *Bondago*, a Dutchman named Willem Nyker, a stolid swinish behemoth. Captain Nyker was interested. At fifty he still felt a warm, pleasant stir at the thought of a native girl of the kind described to him by his yellow cook. A virgin, the cook had assured him, of blinding beauty, very young, who could speak English and who wanted to sail away from India. But, he explained to Captain Nyker, it would be necessary to go carefully at first. She was something extra fine, far better than the girls the *tuan* had known before. Possibly, he hinted, it might be wise to speak of things largely and come to detail when the ship was out to sea. The girl was one who had plenty of flame in her, he went on. He himself had been watching her for some time, with a view to bringing her to the *tuan* when she was ripe, he proceeded glibly.

Captain Nyker glared at him, but without bitterness. "Liar," he grunted. "Yellow peeg! Liar! But pring her oud und I look."

The Malay brought her.

"Yah, ve go dere," Captain Nyker informed Narapatee. He had a good deal of gin in him by that time and was quite amiable. He sat on a canvas chair, and the squidgy fat upon his big face seemed to melt, as though it ran with the sweat. He had put on a dingy coat, once white, with remnants of flaked gold braid hanging to it, and the garment was dank and shapeless with perspiration.

"Vary nize in Angland," he wheezed, grinning genially at the girl. "Und vat you give de Coptan Nyker tak' you to Angland?" he suggested slyly. "Vat you give, eh?"

Narapatee had prepared for this; she was ready to pay for her passage. She fussed for an instant in her bosom and held out her hand. Captain Nyker swayed in his sagging chair, as a preliminary to rising and pulling her to him, before he saw what was in her palm. He tried to stretch out his fat neck, then. An immense ruby and a great diamond flamed and glowed in her palm. His blue eyes turned sharply up at her face and back to the glinting stones again, and his lower jaw bogged down a little. These were signs, not so much of surprise, as of Willem Nyker's cunning at work.

"Val, maybe I do it. Fursht I look at dem." Narapatee laid her treasures in his puffed hand. Nyker was pleasurably excited. The girl had proved, physically, even more than the nigger had promised, and now she was offering him the biggest ruby and the biggest diamond he had ever seen. They must be immensely valuable. They were easily worth more than the vessel, the *Bondago*.

He leaned back suddenly and thrust the jewels into the single wide, deep pocket in his trousers. Its mouth was at the level of his navel and opened about eight inches across. Willem Nyker always had a pocket like that in his trousers; his short arms could not conveniently reach ordinary pockets at the sides. "Yah," he said to Narapatee, "yah; ve go." He was a wealthy man now, he realized. He felt very generously disposed toward the girl as he smiled at her now.

The *Bondago*, miscellaneous cargo, principally tin, hemp and rice, sailed at tide that evening for San Francisco ...

Captain Nyker planned, the first day out, how he was going to slip his ruby and his diamond past American customs. He knew already where he could sell them in San Francisco. The first night out he assaulted Narapatee.

CHAPTER EIGHT

U NTIL the woman drew back into the hall where the yellow rays of the electric light fell on her skin and brought out its dark base, Norris did not realize that she must be the mulatto. Standing on the stoop, in the thin daylight, her skin had been beige-colored. She had a flat, broad face with deep sorrowful eyes. He had only seen her once before and then for a brief instant when he had met Richard Todd emerging from the flat one morning. Richard had, in two dry, hard sentences, explained who and what she was. When she got out of the sunlight, Norris saw, the sorrow faded curiously and her eyes grew cloudy, as if you were looking at the backs of them, as if the fronts had turned inward. Her dress was gray, close to the color of her skin, and that one flat, sad tone was relieved only by a narrow girdle of dull red leather, clasped by an enameled buckle of maroon. She was a tall, straight woman, but even the wooden stiffness of her big bones could not wholly suppress the fine curves at bust and hip and thigh that came to her from her black forbears.

She could not have recognized Norris, yet she sensed that he had some right here, some connection with Richard Todd, for she led the way back into the silent house without a word, without answering Norris' question, without signing that she had heard him. In her movements he could see an inevitabiltiy, not of her own will, but one she felt she was part of, and obeyed. It was disturbing, watching her, for he could not shake off the feeling that this woman had tapped some secret wells of knowledge, possessed power of divination. She was purposeful but resigned, stolid, yet melancholy.

Until Norris sat down and stared at her, she stood against the wall with her hands behind her, silent.

"Richard is dead," she said.

Though he had feared and expected this ever since his mind had cleared, though he had subconsciously known that Richard must already have been buried, still the words cut him across the face, as real as a whipstroke, and he jerked back in pain. There was brutality in the way the mulatto had told him, completely, heavily, hopelessly.

"I am Norris Haldorn," he told her at last.

"Then I got a letter f'you." She took an envelope from a drawer in a table, after pulling aside the fringe of a deep green scarf. There drifted spicily into the room the odor of hot ginger-bread. "Been expectin' you," she said as she handed the letter to him. She went out of the room as Norris unfolded the letter and began to read.

"Norris, my dear fellow:

"The fact that you are reading this means you have come to my house and spoken to Nora. I have told her to make no effort to deliver this letter but to give it to you if you come yourself. I have not been able to understand why you have not come to see me before I go, but I have full faith in your friendship and I esteem you no less because you are not here now. I know your reason for not coming must be valid. I would not write in this positive way—for you may come tomorrow—but the doctor, who is a stout fellow in spite of a dry tongue, has just told me that I probably will not see tomorrow. That's strange because my hand isn't too awfully weak, and I don't feel like I've got a high fever. I feel peculiarly tired, though, and when I finish this I'm going to have the glass of hot rum the medico's promised me and I'm going to doze off for a bit. He tells me, 'I'll be round to see you in the morning.' But I think, from his way of looking at the window when he says it, that I had better write this now if I want to have it written. I think I shall have the rum, now, before I go on.

"I feel sleepier than ever with the hot alcohol inside me; instead of stimulating, it's quieted me ... but I don't need any quieting. I have something rather weird, rather surprising to tell you, and I want my mind to go over it a little more before I turn it into words. Before I tell you about it I want to give you a little advice. My single justification—more a reason, really, than justification— is that I am some years older than you in time and twenty years or so richer in experience. Actually, this isn't going to be advice at all, but just an excuse to let me run my silly thoughts across paper. Don't take what I say too seriously.

"So far as I have been able to discover, Norris, a modified kind of pragmatism is the only philosophy that will work as a system upon which to operate your everyday physical and emotional life. The ideal philosophy, the one that offers the most and appears to me the most inviting, is the living-plan devised by the Roman Catholics, and their faith is the only one marked by beauty and sincerity, but to follow it takes conscious effort, which is more than I will give, or *would* give I ought to say, to the business of getting on. ... Be easy, be good to yourself, then, in every direction that pleases without harming and if it does harm, why, consider carefully now before you decide in this, the youth of your days, to forego any rich experience. When you have grown older, when your resiliency has dried and you're stuffy and musty and sulky, then only the harm in things will appear. I was going to say something about you and me and the campus and some other things but I'm too sleepy and besides, it's all damned sentimental bosh anyhow ... I have to tell you about this other thing.

"One day your father came to see me and asked me if it were true that I was your closest friend, as you'd told him. I said the answer was, yes. He said, then, that he wanted to tell you something but he didn't want you to know it until he was dead; he didn't want it in formal writing as he didn't want to leave a letter. That sounded queer but after he told me what it was, I saw there were good reasons for wanting the information conveyed to you by word of mouth. That was one of the reasons I hoped you would come to see me. Naturally, having kept the word this long, I'm not fool enough to put it on paper now and imperil you. Well, perhaps not imperil, but certainly it is running the risk of injuring you emotionally and ... financially. It has to do with one of three voyages your father made as a young man on a freight steamer sailing out of Portland. I have given the message to Nora, but in such a way that she does not realize its import. When you have finished reading this note, ask Nora to tell you what I told her about Boyd Cable. When she has told you, remember that your father is Boyd Cable. Attach no importance to that name.

"RICHARD TODD."

That abrupt ending jarred Norris; it was not characteristic, he felt, of Dick Todd. He examined the script again; it reminded him of a phonograph running down, slurring, flattening out.

Five minutes passed while Norris read this letter over twice, slowly, and then the mulatto Nora returned. She held out a deep crusted pan, and Norris saw it held a layer of crisp coppery squares of gingerbread. At first this annoyed him, but his annoyance left him when he realized that she was only trying, in her way, to ease his pain. He took a segment of the warm dark bread.

"Nora," he began hesitantly, "you have a message for me regarding ... regarding my friend Boyd Cable. A message that Richard gave you. Remember?"

"Yes," Nora said, and the way she had of drawing out that one word, of pressing its final consonant, made him think of a tube of paste. He saw, when Nora sat down opposite him on a couch covered with tapestried brocade, that she wore no stockings. Her legs were much darker than her face, almost the color of loam.

"Boyd Cable dead an' gone now."

"Yes," Norris responded. "I know."

"Richard"—she made it Ritch-ahd—"told me about Boyd Cable what went off a-sailin' him on a boat. Took hisself a woman in Manila. Went an' married her, too. Hot place, hear tell, that Manila."

"Married her?" Norris echoed, astonished.

"Married her," Nora repeated. "Married her, an' done had a child with her. A son. An' left that woman an' sailed away and didn't come back no more. Boyd Cable nevuh came back no more. Richard want me to tell you. Say you a friend of his'n."

For one wondering instant he fumbled for meanings. *Ed Blackburn.* Was this, then, the reason for the physical resemblance? That came to him first; it was the first rock to come loose under his frantic fingers. Then, other meanings.... A new light on his father, an explanation for Cairn Haldorn's will.... He went back to a consideration of Blackburn. But it was absurd. Ed Blackburn hadn't been a half-breed. But—*God!*—that son would be a legitimate first-born, the real successor to his father's name. And to his estate. But it couldn't be Blackburn. Couldn't it? asked a voice inside him.

"Couldn't it?"

"No, damn it; I say no," he burst out.

Nora said, "You want a drink? Maybe you need a drink."

Norris shook his head. "Tell me the rest of the story."

"Ain't no more story. Richard say thass all."

Thass all ... leaving him groping, befuddled. When Nora got up and turned, her palms showed, butter-colored and a little oily like her legs. She was holding something out to him on one of those yellow discs; a drink. Curious way she held a glass, he thought, flat on her open hand instead of clutched between the fingers. The old haze sank over him for a moment, clouding out everything. Nora's hand laid roughly on his sleeve jerked him back and he stood peering at her with a horrible pain tearing through his head. The old scars across his face began to ache.

"Take a drink. You look sick. Don't be so sad about Richard."

Nora took him out to the cemetery, to Richard's grave. He hated the synthetic quiet of the place. Feathery willow trees bent from hummocks to trail their plumes in too-symmetric ponds. In the ponds ducks floated, and their honking calls, sharp and regular, seemed made by hidden horns. There was, in the very regularity of the place, the unreality, the stiff perfection of a stage setting.

Norris looked at the sentence cut into the ashen-granite stone over Richard's grave. It seemed to him a message from Richard.

MOURN ME NOT

RICHARD TODD

1892——1930

Nora came walking toward him, carrying an armful of crisp pink gladioli; she arranged them in the two tin-lined holes that were sunk in the ground at the foot of the grave, knelt down, and prayed in a whisper, her big-body swaying slowly. The mulatto kept intruding between him and his concern with Richard.

Norris moved away; he left the neat paths and crossed the wide white lawns, acres of them, until he came to a gate in a fence. Through this he walked into an unkempt field full of wild green life. Here grass grew long, and the soil was uneven, rising and falling in swells and lush hollows. Here, he reflected, Richard might better have been buried.

Norris grasped a crumbling clod of black earth and pressed it gently between his fingers; suddenly he crushed it angrily in his fist. He wished, in sudden fury, that he could see the thin cruel head of his dead father before him. He would smash it, by god ... he would pay him back for the senseless sorrow the vanity and morbid bias of the old man had brought down upon him.

How many more invisible dead hands were there upraised powerfully like his father's, clutching at living beings? ... It was as if they had been denied something in life and now reached back for it with petulant fingers. Saint Anthony, he reflected, had reached back like that, but his hand had been sweetly gentle; Cairn Haldorn's hand was harsh and pitiless....

His father had always seemed so dry and so inhuman that it amazed him, when he thought about it later, to learn that Cairn had allowed lust to have its way with him, even in early man-hood. The fact of the trips at sea, too, had surprised Norris.

Standing in the station, waiting for the train, the fog in his chaotic grief began to thin; one ironic wind blew stronger at it than any other ... the thought that the plans Cairn Haldorn had so carefully prepared had defeated with utter completeness every object they were expected to achieve. Norris smiled now, thinking of his perturbation over the story relayed to him by the mulatto Nora. He had almost forgotten about her, as an indi-vidual. She came up to the station now and stood beside him on the platform. She didn't ask him why he had gone away.

"Thought I'd fin' you here," Nora said. "Forgot one more thing. Richard tell me that woman of Boyd Cable's a white woman. He marry her in Manila, but she wa'n't no Manila girl. English woman, he say."

She walked away and he had a final flash of those lemon-colored palms as she swung her hands in a long arc behind her.

Inside the station there was a newspaper rack leaning against the bench; in it were two papers. Norris pulled one of them out and held it before him. It was *The World*, the issue dated eight days ago. His eyes scanned the front page, seeing nothing. He started to turn the page when his eyes sent an incredible message to his brain. He turned back to the front page and looked again. This time he saw it:

NORRIS HALDORN, SON OF OIL
BARON AND HEIR TO FORTUNE,
SUICIDE IN SAN FRANCISCO

Financial and Social World Stunned by
Death of Youthful Scion of
Famous New York Family

AUTHORITIES ARE PUZZLED

SAN FRANCISCO, June 2. (A.P.)—The body of Norris Haldorn, youthful master of the gigantic Empire-Haldorn petroleum interests, was found tonight in a room on the third floor of the fashionable Hotel De Soto. He had apparently shot himself through the head.

The tragedy occurred presumably during a telephone call, since the receiver was down and attendants who rushed in after hearing the shot found the line open.

There was some interval of time between the report of the shot and discovery of the body. Police discovered the reason for this in the fact that the room where the tragic affair took place was a little-used conference hall, set at the far end of the building. It had not been used for months, hotel attaches declared.

There was no note to indicate a possible motive for young Haldorn taking his own life. The revolver, a small caliber gun, was found lying near his outstretched hand with one shot fired.

Police, after questioning the widow, a bride of four months, announced they were at a loss to account for the shooting. Mrs. Haldorn collapsed when informed of her husband's death. She was the former Miss Night Gambier, leader in the younger social set of New York City.

James Bartlett, captain of Haldorn's palatial steam yacht, and said to be a close friend, was unable to offer any explanation for the death of his employer. So far as detectives were able to discover, young Haldorn had been nervous and excited of late, but not despondent. He had come here recently following a lengthy tour of the coast of

India and South China in his yacht in accord with terms of his father's extraordinary will which commanded Haldorn to travel abroad for four years unless he married within that time, before coming into actual mastery of the enormous fortune amassed by Cairn Haldorn who founded the Empire Petroleum Corporation.

Police said they had traced the telephone call from the "death room" to a residence in the Marina district but refused to disclose whether they had obtained a definite clue that would lead to a solution of the mysterious shooting.

Haldorn, it was known, recently purchased the Van Ryan country home in Hillsborough and had taken up temporary residence there following ..."

The story wound on, crawling down the page, to an enigmatic conclusion.

To say that Ed Blackburn had committed suicide was, Norris thought, absurd. The whole affair seemed so impossible. It just couldn't be. It was a fraud, a catastrophic fairy tale. Then he saw a copy of the current noon edition tabloid *Graphic* whose headline, smeared black over a full page photograph of himself, screamed:

HINT HALDORN SLAIN

New Disclosures in Exclusive Graphic
Story Show Tuesday's Tragedy
May Have Been Murder

SAN FRANCISCO, June 9. (Exclusive).—Revelations today in the Haldorn shooting that took the life a week ago of the multimillionaire "crown prince of petroleum" indicated the possibility of murder....

The photograph, Norris remembered, was one that had been taken at the polo matches, two years before. There had been a kind of questing wonder in his face at the time. He had changed so much since then ... so much.

The things Norris did next, in a furious burst of energy, he did almost automatically, as though to free himself....

He sent a telegram to the chief of police in San Francisco, signing himself Stoner Young. As personal attorney for Haldorn, he was leaving at once by plane to aid in the investigation. Norris began to realize that to evade the issue now was to force himself, inevitably, into oblivion forever.

He stopped, appalled. Good god, had he read that aright? Nervously, he flipped the *World* open again. There it was "... the former Miss Night Gambier...." Then Ed Blackburn had married Night. The full implications of this fact gathered in his mind slowly. He continued walking to the air transport office. There were damned good reasons, of course, why Blackburn should want to marry Night.

With her as his wife, the likelihood was minimized that she would expose him and suffer herself the consequent ignominy and humiliation. That would—if this judgment of the girl was accurate—insure him against treachery from her. And what so logical, his mind suggested casually, as a murder when the regal, the imperious young Night found who and what her husband was? Norris played with the thought, twirling it about in his mind like a bright cane. And presently, though it annoyed him to think so, he knew he was jealous....

He was aware that the clerk was staring at him curiously.

"Did you say the name was Haldorn?"

Norris laughed. "No, no; I'm afraid I was thinking about that story in the papers. My name is Stoner Young."

The clerk scribbled on the pad in front of him. "You're lucky. That's the last seat left. Plane leaves at three o'clock. Thank you, Mr. Young."

At his hotel Norris packed carelessly. It would be amusing, he thought as he started for the plane, to go among his friends, now that he was presumably dead; he was like a character in one of those stories of revival after burial. It might be amusing but it would also be ghastly. It gave him a sense of strange power, this thought that he was of the living dead, a wraith.

He, whom the world accepted as dead, was coming sprawling through space, still with a mortal body. He was death and life, more than the one, assuredly less than the other, like the scarlet hibiscus that, impaled on a bamboo stalk in a bowl, has life but is not alive and will collapse and wither with the twilight.

When the plane pulled itself over Diablo's smooth hump and settled down on Oakland Airport, Norris was glad. The trip had been tiresome—endless miles of an endless map that unrolled jerkily far below, checkerboards of brown and green that gave interminably on checker-boards of black and gray.

He came out of the plane to find William Eight in the little group on the field awaiting the passengers.

William Eight was only a patrolman most of the time, a harness bull, and a poor one, at that, since his stature was short and his physique frail, and his eyes had the goggling guilelessness of an infant crowing over a rattle. But he knew that his superiors had found him possessed of a useful tact and aplomb on the occasions when it was necessary officially to welcome a celebrity; and a good many and various persons were categoried as celebrities.

"A lawyer for the Haldorn outfit," the chief had said to Eight, "is pretty much of a somebody. Bound to be. But it wouldn't look right to go down myself. You go. And mind what you say, Bill."

To Norris, now, in his best non-committal monotone, William Eight said, "Let me welcome you to the city on behalf of the police department."

Until the ferry had withdrawn her splintered chest from the mole and bustled out onto the wind-whipped blue bay, Norris was silent. Then he asked, "You have a definite lead in the suicide yet?"

"Suicide?" William Eight couldn't resist going on. "That was no suicide, Mr. Young; that was murder. Out and out murder."

The bullet hole, he explained, had been in the center of Mr. Haldorn's forehead, a place the wound couldn't be if he'd shot himself.

The skyline, ahead, grew slowly out of the thick summer haze. The vapors from the salt water made new wine sharp on the wind. When the boat passed the chalky cliff off Yerba Buena, the haze had receded and tall buildings appeared clear against the sky. Most of his weariness, Norris noticed with elation, had fallen away from him; a man could feel free here.

The gulls, iridescent curved planes, sounded their high, hollow call as they swooped by; the noise increased in volume when the cook turned a full pail of bread crusts over the aft rail of the ferry.

CHAPTER NINE

THE De Soto, Norris found, rose to thirty stories of neo-Spanish grandeur, as if the builders had taken one of the suburban *casas* of adobe and tiles and patio and sudden porches and, applying giant lips, had blown it up to this skyscraper size. Walking through it, Norris came upon clusters of dark glossy rafters, massive and impressive, in places where they didn't, architecturally, belong. The walls, inside, were of a chalky cream color, left rough to simulate the pebbled texture of honest adobe; they were relieved, in the lobby, by alcoves hung, incongruously, with long, narrow gilt-banded French mirrors. At the rear of the lobby was a patio, and in that was a fountain spurting into a pool decorated with ribald Italian statuary. Around all this, like a patchwork lining, were innumerable little shops, each bearing a different decorative scheme on its front. It was disappointing to find this kind of vulgar show in a city he had always thought of as mellow with the age of tolerant years. But his irritation was really with Ed Blackburn, with the Blackburn represented for him by this garish place.

Norris took a room in the hotel but went to it only to put his bags in the closet. It was reasonable to suppose that detectives would still be around and that agents of one or two of Empire's most important competitors would, like ghouls, be prowling about. He decided to test a plan that had come to him in the plane.

He went down to the barber shop and aroused it from its early-afternoon torpor by getting into one of the marble-armed chairs. As he settled back in the chair, he thought of Night and made up his mind to go down to Hillsborough to see her that very evening. He might as well acclimate himself as quickly as possible. For one thing, he wanted to find out what Blackburn's activities had been. Assuming that Blackburn had been killed by some one who believed him to be Norris Haldorn, then, if Norris resumed his own identity, that person might strike again. He smiled grimly to himself at the thought that he still had some expectations of reclaiming his own name; how utterly hopeless it seemed.

The barber's scissors stopped their metallic *sluff-sluff-sluff.* Norris said, casually, "That shooting here—mighty queer, wasn't it?" Perhaps he could pick up some threads of gossip in this way. The barber nodded his head a few times before he spoke.

"Yeah, yeah, yeah." Like a phonograph needle caught in a groove. "Certain'y was, yeah. Certain'y was. Yup." The barber continued nodding his head in silence, but offered no further revelations.

Back in his room, Norris called for a bellhop. These messengers were supposed to be an autonomous secret service in hotels. The bellhop, presumably, knew everything that went on among the lodgers. Norris took a twenty dollar note from his wallet and put it into an envelope, leaving the end of the bill visible.

The bellhop came in, a short man with a dry, hard face.

"Sit down, I want to talk to you."

"Yessir, thankye." The bellhop noticed the envelope and stared at it as he sat down.

"I want some information. I'll pay you well. I'm not a detective; if you tell me anything, I'll forget where it came from. If I'm ever asked, I have never seen you."

"Whatta ya want?" the voice sounded weary; the eyes were suspicious. "Is it that shootin' business? That Haldorn thing?"

Norris looked out of the window, over the acres of roofs. "Yes, that's it. Do you know anything about it?"

"You a relative?"

"No."

"You're no detective; I know that m'self. Newspaper reporter?"

"No."

"Well—I need a hundred dollars."

"Fifty now and fifty when I've heard it."

He took the money and put it into the pocket of his maroon trousers. "You go down to Nine-Twen'y-Four. Door ain't locked. You go in and say, 'Well, Dalt; are you feelin' better today?' Say that to him, see? This bird's name is Dalt Acres. When he asks you who you are, tell him you're Norris Haldorn. He won't be able to see you. He's got the blinds over his eyes. They's a big bandage wrapped around his head and he can't see anything. His eyes is all through. Bum gin done it. He was awful chummy with this Haldorn guy and he don't know Haldorn's dead. Just between you an' me and the bedpost there, this bird Acres just woke up this mornin'. He's been out like a light for a week."

"How do you know this?" Norris tried to suppress the excitement he felt.

"I been fetchin' medicine up to the room. Medicine an' stuff. I know what I'm talkin' about. This Dalt Acres and that Haldorn batted around together a lot. Acres'll prob'ly spill plenty when you walk in; he'll feel like talkin', too."

Ten minutes later, Norris went down in the elevator to the ninth floor. He lit a cigarette as he started to walk through the hall. He opened the door of room 924 and was about to step in when he had to twist and flatten himself against the wall. Two men were wheeling a gurney toward him—they were moving a man with a bandage around his head. He lay still.

"I'm a friend of his and—" Norris began.

"Too late. Convulsions," the man nearest Norris grunted, without slackening his pace. "It's a coma now. He won't come out of this. I've seen 'em before an' I know. Booze-fighter."

Norris, when they had disappeared down the corridor, entered Dalt Acres' room. A maid, with an air of awful weariness, was painfully pulling the sheets from the bed. "You're too late," she said dully. "They took him away." She waved a hand toward the bureau. "I guess that's for you."

It was a sealed envelope, addressed with the single word "Haldorn" and done in letters so large that they covered the whole front of it. The script wavered and staggered. It was the handwriting of a man who could not see what he was doing, and who was also weak, physically. Norris pulled out the smeared, ink-spattered sheet inside and began to read it.

"Look out for that God damned wife of yours. She knows too much about you. Your friend Dalt."

Norris looked at the note for a long time, leaning against the bureau. The maid, he finally realized, was talking to him.

"You feel sick? You look kinda pale. You want me to get you something?" She was leaning on the handle of her carpet sweeper, regarding him with tired eyes.

Norris shook his head as he went out.

CHAPTER TEN

NORRIS stood at the window of a long dim room, waiting. A servant had told him that Mrs. Haldorn or her mother would be down soon to receive him. He knew he ought to be busy concocting answers to the questions they might ask him; but his mind refused to consider anything but the incredible and fantastic fact that he was seeking his own murderer. What a strange thing it was—to be hunting one's own murderer. He wondered how Night would receive him. What would she say? Could she possibly suspect who he was? Did she know who killed Blackburn? Could she have discovered Blackburn's real identity? He stared out through the French windows. The house and gardens were set in Hillsborough, a suburb south of San Francisco. Hedges and rows of drooping eucalypti hid the people who lived here. The estate was bordered on one side by the ocean, and, on the other, by El Camino Real, over which there flowed an unending procession of fast-moving automobiles.

To the east, on the bridge which spanned the bay, lights hung like glow worms pinned up against the sky. Behind these, across the bay, ladders of lamps in the Alameda homes climbed the gentle hills.

Nostalgia seized Norris, a fierce longing to be himself, in the surroundings he knew and loved ... to do the things he wanted to do, and to say what he wished without fear of the consequences of each utterance. He wanted, above all else, to do or say something, when Night faced him, so characteristic of himself that she would know at once that she was in the presence of Norris Haldorn. But he could think of nothing, no gesture or turn of phrase, that was unique unto himself. He was shocked to discover this. It meant that he could not reveal his identity to Night; if he did she would not believe him. He decided not to try.

Passing through the hall on his way to this dim room, Norris had noticed that Lucia Gambier had already begun to leave her mark upon this place. She had a passion for small, live things. The rooms seemed crowded with goldfish bowls and bird cages. Her own fecundity having died, she had resorted to vicarious maternity in this way. Strange that she should have given birth to Night. How unlike each other Night and her mother were.

He heard footsteps clicking down the stairs and tried to think of a convincing opening speech. He would have to speak warily, he knew, for it was certain that a message had been sent by the attorneys themselves, probably by Mary Granch.

Except for a small lamp under a parchment shade that sent a crescent of soft amber light from its upturned horn, the room now was quite dark. Night, entering, lit the chandelier; under its blanched, chilly brilliance she appeared warm, glowing. She wore a shining gown of bright beryl and a chiffon scarf, lighter in color. Her head, framed by that astonishing hair of jonquil-yellow, was like a flower—a daffodil on a smooth polished green stalk. Norris tried to read significance into her failure to wear widow's black.

Had she, he asked, received his telegram?

"Your telegram?" Her voice seemed curiously small and cold for so much physical radiance. "Your telegram? I suppose it's among the thousand others. After the fifth or sixth I stopped reading them." Norris looked at her calmly, without speaking. Now that she was here, he no longer felt the need to speak; rather, he felt it was she who should speak. She asked, "Did I understand that you are connected with the Empire legal staff? I mean, my maid said something—that is—in announcing you—about your—"

Norris answered stiffly, "Yes, that's right." The part of his mind that he could not control, was obscurely throbbing somewhere inside him; he could sense it in the faint eddies of desire that swirled about in his consciousness. Meanwhile he tried to read from her face, her gestures, her voice, the truth about her relations with Ed Blackburn.

"Were you ever aboard the *Troubadour?*" she was asking. Norris nodded. Night went on, "Yes, I was sure I had seen you before. It's queer to know you, and yet not to, like that."

"How is your mother?"

"Still very nervous. Why did they send you, too? I mean, there are four lawyers here already, living here in the house, and a lot of others who are up in San Francisco." There was something of real mirth in her smile. "I don't mean to be harsh—only, well …"

"Oh, I shan't be staying here," Norris assured her hastily. Obviously, she meant he couldn't stay. Her attitude was baffling. Her nervousness might be due to restrained grief, but it might also be caused by her attempt to posture an attitude of grief she really didn't feel. And why did she seem so apprehensive? Did she finally discover who her husband was? What fury must have flamed in her when she found out the truth, when she realized that she had given her lovely body to a shallow, shiftless impostor, a fugitive from justice, sick, greedy and untutored.

"I think we'll go to Italy to rest as soon as these legal details are over," she was saying. "I don't mean to say anything critical of lawyers—I suppose you can't help the delays that come up—but I hope you and the other gentlemen get matters settled quickly. Not for myself so much, as for my mother."

Despite her last remark, Night appeared in no haste to end the conversation. She settled back comfortably in her chair and began to question him languidly. He knew that somewhere in the room there must be a great bowl of fresh roses. While she talked, his eyes caressed her breasts in admiration. She was so lusciously formed; it was pleasant to sit here and watch the soft, quick movements of her lips as she spoke, the gestures of her hands, the undulations of her body.

"It's terrifying to know you're so young and feel so old." She said this seriously, as though there were deeper implications than the words revealed. Norris was abruptly alert.

"I can't say because I—"

Night interrupted, "You can't say because you've never been either young or old. I can tell that much about you. But I've been both. I'm beginning to think that the only joy worth while is serenity, an untroubled mind, even if it means a mind empty of—of ... oh, empty of hope and of hate or—well, turbulence of any kind."

Norris, moved by the cautious need to stay in character, asked, "Have arrangements been concluded for probating the will?"

"Oh, I don't want to talk about any of those things. Why should I be bothered, since all you bright attorneys are being paid to attend to them?" She had interlaced her fingers and placed them behind her head.

"You know, it's a curious thing," she smiled at him, "but of all the officials who have come here since—since *that* happened— you are the ugliest, the most taciturn, and the only one I want to talk to."

Anger and shame flushed his scarred face and made Norris even more cruelly aware of his disfigurement. Damn her! Did she have to speak about his face? It was the first time that anyone had said anything about it in his presence. What would she have said, he wondered, if he had been able to speak with his own voice instead of with a voice thickened, blurred and mutilated?

Whatever it was Night had intended to say to him, he never heard it. A maid came in to announce that Mr. Young was wanted on the telephone. When he returned, Night was gone. The call had come from the captain of the detective bureau in San Francisco.

"I'm calling you because we have something special on for tonight and thought you might like to follow the progress of the investigation personally. We understand that you're handling the police end of the legal work."

"That's right. I'd like to be in on any new developments. What's scheduled?"

"We're going aboard the *Johanna Jones* tonight. We'll send a car for you if you want to come along."

"Fine. I'll be glad to go with you."

"Okay. Be ready at eight."

The maid said to Norris, on his way out: "Mrs. Haldorn asked me to tell you she would like you to have a room here, sir."

Norris looked blankly at the maid. "Mrs. Haldorn wants me to stay here?"

"Yes sir, she wants to speak with you at ten in the morning."

"At ten?"

"Yes sir, that's what she said."

"*Hm-mm!* Certainly, I'll stay if she wishes. Thank Mrs. Haldorn for me. But please explain, if I am late, that I was kept out on business tonight, and could not, for that reason, be up by ten. I may not get back until dawn, you see."

"Yes sir, I'll tell her."

CHAPTER ELEVEN

NORRIS wished he had a stiff drink. Waiting on the pier with William Eight under a cold blanket of fog, Norris wished he had a drink of brandy or whiskey,—something that would go down hot and sharp.

Somewhere in the north the Point lighthouse hooted its mournful call, a long wailing sound as if it were in pain. On nights such as this, the light was useless. The hissing wash of the breakers, farther back where the sea met the sand, sounded like the seething of a huge cauldron giving off steam.

The fog dulled the sounds of the night and the sea; it muffled everything with its soft gray folds. It made all sounds curiously remote and flat. Even the *thput-thput-thput* of the motor boat exhaust became a muted throbbing.

The noise of the exhaust became sharper and lighter; its beat slowed down. The boat must be close now, down below on the water. It had stopped moving. Norris went to the edge and looked over the dark, crusted piles. Staring through the choking mist, he made out the contours of a speedboat. The fog did not depress him; rather, he was buoyed up by the thought of what might lie ahead.

They hooted at the driver of the boat and he backed it up and pulled it against the landing that floated on pontoons at the bottom of the long incline.

"Might as well start right off," Eight told the driver. "Nobody else coming on this run on a night like this."

"Don't fool yourself," the driver answered, grinning. "It may be a hell of a night, but there are a lot of people out."

The boat rocked a little at first as she slid over the water but she gradually settled down to smooth, steady going. She was a fast boat. The pier and the San Mateo coast had faded into the fog. Out here, even with a wet, salt wind, there persisted the strong vegetable odor of the Moss Beach cabbage farms. After a while, that too was gone. The boat was a point in space, moving against a constantly receding gray wall of cold smoke.

William Eight looked at his wrist watch. "Just midnight." He turned to the driver, "Trip going to take longer tonight?"

"Yeah," the pilot growled, and his cigarette fell from his mouth to the water on the floor of the boat. Norris offered him another. The pilot accepted and, after a few puffs, softened his tone as he said: "Too much of a crowd out there tonight to suit me. On a stinking night like this. Too many men without women too. Might be a little trouble."

Out ahead lay the *Johanna Jones*, most infamous of all the floating gambling halls that infested the California coast. Her stacks, William Eight had explained, were innocent of smoke, and not a pound of steam had rattled in her rusting boilers for a year. Once she had cut the water, bearing honest cargoes in her hold and on her decks: coffee, rice, wheat, machinery—but no more. Despoiled of her motors, she lay still upon the sea. When she moved, as she did only when ocean currents or weather demanded, she plugged along at the end of a line thrown by a tug summoned from the harbor.

The speedboat was nuzzling her side before Norris saw the old ship in the fog. The *Johanna Jones* moved so little—for her hold was weighted down with an accumulation of scrap iron— that it seemed her keel squatted right on the ocean bottom.

The thin brassy twanging of a jazz orchestra sprayed on Norris' ears as he climbed aboard the *Johanna Jones*,—a weird and incongruous medley out here on the open ocean.

"The music," said William Eight, "is pretty fair out here."

"It's not music."

"Even so," William Eight insisted, "it's pretty fair."

"Well,—" Officer Eight leaned against the bar and began peacefully to swallow a glass of milk. His large round eyes were bland and lamblike. "I have been out to this ship before. The milk is very rich here," he announced slowly.

Norris did not answer him, but as he looked around he realized that of the twelve or fourteen men along the bar, ten must be detectives. Something in their postures, the cast of their faces told him. Besides, they lingered over soft drinks, unlike the regular customers.

Looking into the mirror behind the bar, Norris had his first glimpse of Kid Rollers, born Hymie Gold. His head was shaped like a pumpkin, bulging at the temples. Two streaks of bald scalp left a furrow of black hair down the center of his head. Below his eyes, the skin was creased and pouched. He was twisting a cigar between his large, sensuous lips. His huge chest swelled tight against his formal evening shirt; below it billowed a colossal belly. And that was all. He had no legs.

Hymie Gold had no legs. He had left them, one rainy night, on the gravel road between Crescent City and Eureka, while the bloody rest of him got away in a car headed north, barely missing the last barrage from the submachine gun of the hijackers. Hymie had descended from the convoy car in a frenzy of anger to meet the gentlemen under Eddie De Pano. Stumbling on a stone, he had fallen to the ground where the sharp chains on the wheels of De Pano's truck had removed his legs. The noise of it, which he would always remember beyond the pain, had been a soggy crunching. Eddie De Pano had profited to the extent of three truckloads of very poor whiskey.

Some time thereafter, behind the China Beach Warehouse, under a packing box, the body of De Pano had been discovered with thirty-four bullets in it—a very untidy but still a thorough piece of work. De Pano was duly buried, while Hymie Gold came out of the hospital to oversee the operations of the *Johanna Jones*. He moved about on a specially-constructed wheel chair, all done in blue plush with scarlet fringe, with real balloon tires on the high wheels. He made occasional visits to shore to confer with other bootleggers, but these trips were infrequent because it pained his pride to be wheeled about like an infant in a pram in view of those who disliked him and, perhaps, envied him his possessions.

The gaming tables were at the other end of the untidy room; there was too much conversation, however, for really heavy gambling. Watching Kid Rollers in the mirror, Norris saw a stocky man with an Irish face lean against the back of the wheel chair and say something to him.

"Go away and don't bother me," Hymie shouted irritably, as though he wanted to call attention to the other man. "I don't give no cuts out here to grafting cops. I only pay for protection where I need it."

"I only said I was a police officer."

"I heard you the first time and I knew it without you telling me, McMoyle."

"Then we understand each other. This is a raid and you're under arrest."

"Raid?" Hymie asked, puzzled. "For what? I ain't under your jurisdiction out here. This is the open sea."

The players about the tables, with few exceptions,—probably employees of Hymie's,—went on playing and ignored the disturbance. McMoyle said something in Hymie's face which Norris didn't hear. Hymie said, "Sure I'll go; why, sure. Answer all the questions you want."

On the way ashore, William Eight told Norris why they were paying so much attention to the conductor of the *Johanna Jones.* "Hymie Gold was talking to Norris Haldorn by telephone when Norris Haldorn was shot."

"Do they suspect he had something to do with it?"

"Maybe, at any rate the telephone line was open when the murder was committed. Hymie must have heard whatever words were spoken and whatever sounds were made in the room at the time."

At the dock an altercation arose because Hymie was unwilling to leave his wheel chair. Norris noticed a sudden change of demeanor on the part of McMoyle and his detectives, now that they were ashore. One of them pushed his open hand against Hymie Gold's face and held it there, while he said to McMoyle, "Shove him in the back seat?"

They threw him onto the leather seat in the back of their touring car. He had been noisy and full of oaths during the argument, but now, except for an occasional hiss of cursing under his breath, he was silent. Norris sat in front while they drove on to San Francisco. Again he thought how strange it was to be seeking the man who had taken his life. What if he should find this man? Or perhaps it was a woman? Would this murderer make another attempt to kill him when he discovered that he, Haldorn, was still alive?

Except for Hymie saying "Lousy damned bastards," behind him, periodically, nothing varied the even drone of the motor as the car came north through Colma and onto the long hills of

Mission Street. A feeling of satisfaction that he could be a specta-
tor to all this surged up in Norris. When the car stopped before
the ugly gray front of the Hall of Justice, he saw a patrolman with
a beetred face kicking a man up the stairs. The detectives carried Hymie in. It hurt Hymie's pride to be carried, worse than it
pained him to be wheeled, and he demanded angrily that he be
set down so that he might roll himself along on the ball-bear-
inged wheels hitched to his underparts.

"Can't do that, Kid," McMoyle told him. "The noise might
wake up the babies."

"All right," Hymie agreed, with what must have been remarkable restraint for him. He should have let Mealy and Johnny and
Brats come with him, he realized that now. It was too late to
wish they were here; he had ordered them to stay on the boat. He
decided, now, to make no breaks.

When the officers carried him down the dirty marble corridor, they might have been bearing a huge idol, so flat and immobile were his face and body. The light from the hanging lamps,
reflected by the marble chips in the mosaic on the walls, painted
weird blue streaks across his face. It was a face of paste, stippled
with black stubble. Norris looked at Hymie Gold and saw that he
had closed his eyes. Hymie was thinking of his girl.

Kid Rollers had picked a long, lissome girl out of the city, a girl
with curious oval thighs and high breasts who had decided that
the luxury Hymie Gold offered her was preferable to a smelly
hotel room and working as a model in Tarnahoff's. And she had
thought it reasonable that Hymie would—as she phrased it to
herself—be handing in his pass-book to the chief teller and closing out his account one of these days, when she would be due
for all of his possessions. He had, before she had agreed to come
to him, shown her a will, signed and witnessed and recorded,

bequeathing her all of his property. She hadn't been willing to accept that; a gift deed, undated, would be much better, she had told him. She had been given the deed.

So she had come to his suite on the *Johanna Jones* and there she served his wishes.

Hymie gave orders to her from a pedestal of glossy Carrara dolomite which he had bought for himself. He used to sit on this pedestal like a statue, with the girl in front of him. Sometimes the daïs seemed about to walk off by itself; at other times the squat figure on top appeared to have fused with and become a part of the lifeless marble base; for the wonder of it was that Hymie Gold had ordered the thing carved in the shape of a pair of legs, planted well apart. Perched on top of these staunch long limbs, he looked almost heroic,—for Hymie had a big upper body and when he drew it up straight and tautened all of its soft flesh he seemed a symbol of mighty power. His own legs had been round, bowed and knotty; these, however, were a splendid pair of limbs, such as a marathon runner might have. God had taken Hymie's legs away so Hymie had given himself a new and better pair. He was a new kind of centaur, with the head of a monster, the body of a man and the limbs of a god. And often, when his woman took note to admire the figure he made in the center of the room, Hymie would be so pleased that, closing his eyes, he would feel the alabaster legs throbbing under him warm with life, ready to take him striding out of the room. It was not difficult for him to believe this, for, though his legs were gone, his brain held intact the vivid memory of how they felt. Besides, didn't his legs actually ache when it was cold? Hymie needed no other proof to lull his reason into acceptance of the miracle.

Between Hymie and the stone legs there was a lubricated swivel so that Hymie could swing himself around at will. But he did not use this often, since it disassociated him immediately from his make-believe limbs; when the upper half of him moved, he felt the drag of the dead weight below.

It was Hymie Gold's custom, when the subject came up, to remark that he had the finest pair of legs in the world. And, in a sense, he was speaking the truth, for these legs of his never grew weary as did those of other men; they stood all day and all night and never bent for rest or flexed for ease. They held him high as tirelessly at the end of four hours as when he first settled upon them, and as well now, after nine years, as the day the sculptor had delivered them to the *Johanna Jones*. What other man's legs could stand so long and never curl for sleep? Hymie Gold was rightfully proud of his legs.

The hours Kid Rollers enjoyed most were those, when saddled atop his resplendent limbs, he would speak of his plans to his girl. No matter what she thought, she never disagreed; she displayed flattering attention always, and sometimes, at his wish, her body.

Such exemplary conduct earned for her the confidence and even the affection of Hymie Gold, as far as Hymie could cherish anyone but himself. Hymie Gold trusted her. That was vital for her safety as well as his own peace of mind; all in all, the arrangement worked well for both of them.

Very precious to him were those occasions when she pirouetted undraped before him. He sat, at such times, with his eyes half-closed as if to hold her shimmering beauty in his mind. Always these performances would be followed by a mad and lustful frenzy when, her posturing ended, she wheeled him to the couch and helped him off his pedestal. And there his legs would stand, eager to be off, chaste, white and vigorous, while he lay with his woman on the soft couch. In this way, Hymie Gold's legs of Carrara dolomite, with the shine of young ivory in their whiteness, gradually became associated in his mind with the ultimate in pleasure; eventually they became, as later all legs became, his symbol for rapture.

Here in the Hall of Justice, however, there were no marble legs. They piled Hymie on top of a desk, propping him up like a sack of onions. The Kid waited for them to begin. But McMoyle merely explained, in a few curt words, why Stoner Young was among them. Then he turned out the lights and they all filed out quietly, Norris silent and perplexed. McMoyle then closed the door, leaving Hymie Gold alone in the dark.

Hymie looked about him. The room was cold and bare; in the dim moonlight he could see a dozen old desks and chairs, as though it had served as a classroom of some kind. Outside, the wind moaned as it swept around the corner of the building; occasionally it rattled the windows.

"Dirty skunks," muttered Hymie, with feeling. That helped a little, but its effect soon wore off. He was a prisoner on the desk. It was three feet to the floor, too far for him to drop. Unlike some legless men, he did not have strong, agile arms,—exercise had never been part of his program of existence—now he couldn't lower himself. Falling was out of the question: it is one thing to drop three feet and land easily on the balls of your feet, but something else again to land on your tender midsection, especially with a pair of steel wheels tied underneath you. Anyhow, why should he attempt to get down? He was tired, and this was as good a time as any to try and catch up on some lost sleep. He tried to sleep.

His chin began to pinch his neck as he nodded and his chest began to ache; there was nothing against which he could rest his tortured back.

Besides, he was thirsty. Across the room, barely visible, stood a ten gallon bottle of water upturned in an icing jug. A tall, frosted tumbler was underneath the tap. Moisture had congealed, like a jacket of silver lace, upon the bottle. His tongue was dry; he could hardly swallow.

Hymie had a plan. He would pull out the drawers of the desk and use them as props in getting down to the floor. Then he would roll over to that tap, let the cold water fill the tumbler, and drink it by pressing the tumbler to his lips. But when he tried the drawers he found they were locked. He couldn't budge them.

"Dirty, lousy skunks," Hymie reflected. He was desperately thirsty.

He forbore to call out for help, principally out of pride. He tried wheeling himself backward to the edge of the desk, intending to drop off and break the fall with his hands. But he stopped each time just as he felt himself beginning to tip over the edge. He was afraid to try it. He knew he would hit the floor very hard. If only he could get hold of a telephone. What a damned fool he had been to come alone. He'd know better after this. *Lice*, that's what they were to play a trick like this. *Dirty* lice.

Hymie Gold was being softened.

CHAPTER TWELVE

H YMIE was surprised; surprised that they had brought him back to the *Johanna Jones*. They had really done nothing to him. He had expected, from the fury of their questioning, that they would lock him in a cell, charged with one of those vague conspiracy crimes. They had done that to Willie Hurdels, he remembered. The process, as Hymie recalled it, was to use a pair of informers. *Informers!* Stoolies was what they were, he thought bitterly. They'd swear to anything at the trial and then afterwards they would spend a few weeks in some outlying county jail to kill the scent before they started out again.

"Skunks I" Hymie yelled helplessly at the detectives as they set him down flush on the desk. He glared up at them.

"You'd steal the wax out of a woman's ears," he screamed. Apparently that wasn't much of a crime; the detectives laughed.

Kid Rollers was no fool; he wouldn't do anything drastic now, even to salve his pride. He got himself hoisted into his red plush chair, wheeled to his own room, and set upon his stone legs. There, head down in a Napoleonic pose, he sat thoughtfully and drank whiskey. He consoled himself with the knowledge that he had given the "dicks" nothing. "Not a damn' thing out of me," he grunted aloud.

Weary and puzzled, Norris returned to Hillsborough. As he started back, the sun began to send a flood of warm, yellow morning light over miles of bright gardens and fields. In the garden, the welcome peace of shining gold and green lulled and soothed him. Norris stopped and sat down, grateful for the gentle, serene warmth. A big chipmunk shot across the grass at his right and for a second Norris thought it flashed a tiny sword. Then he saw that it was only a long blade of grass before which the animal had stopped with paws uplifted. Norris lay back and put his hands under his head and stared at the gentle blue of the sky. The grass was thick and high and swayed with the wind.

He lay there, stirred by wonder, touched by a faint sense of anticipation, by an obscure belief that understanding was about to wash over him.... His eyes closed ... he was so sleepy ... a man like him had married Night ... a man like him was dead ... his father....

Later, when he went up into the house, he learned that the four lawyers had gone to Los Angeles to attend a conference with Andrew Clarke, managing director of Empire. That meant he wouldn't be disturbed for at least another day.

CHAPTER THIRTEEN

HYMIE Gold turned over on his bed. The pain across his stomach seemed to have let up a little. The liquor must have done that. He reached out again for the bottle. He felt grateful to the brandy; grateful to the man who had made it, and to any one who had ever had anything to do with it. It, alone, had been able to ease this aching misery within him.

Suddenly the darkness became oppressive. He pressed the button on the wall next to his bed and a dozen hidden lamps began to glow about the room. This was Hymie's conception of elegance. The finest speakeasy he had ever seen, Brancosi's near San Bruno, had delighted him with just such a display of subdued lamps. Glaring lights had therefore become identified, for Hymie, with a class of humans and a class of objects vaguely covered in his mind by the label "tinhorn." It was a word of which he was very fond. Decidedly, he did not want his own chambers aboard the *Johanna Jones* to be tinhorn. So his bedroom and the four rooms adjoining it, which he used, had suddenly acquired warm bright electric eggs under parchment, with silk shades of apricot and scarlet and cobalt. There were no green shades. Hymie disliked green. Why, he could not say. He knew only that it displeased him as, now, the brandy pleased him.

After taking a drink, Hymie lay back on the pillows and held the bottle up over his eyes, like a baby holding a toy, staring at it gravely with blank eyes. He thought, fleetingly, of Stoner Young and of Haldorn. His thought pattern now, as always, was a composite of innumerable small details. He remembered the jewels he had put into the wall safe two hours ago, just before he had gone to bed. Then he thought of Bill Nyker. *There* was a tinhorn, he reflected,—that dumb bastard Nyker. He had known even before last night that Bill Nyker was dumb. Why, any guy who drinks when he gambles, especially when he gambles for heavy money, is nothing but a bum. Of course, he had cheated those stones, that big diamond and that large ruby, from Nyker,—but after all, it couldn't have happened if Nyker hadn't been drunk. The fool could only blame himself. Served him right. The two gems, bound together by gold claws, had looked damned swell on the palm of his hand. A glow of satisfaction suffused Hymie at the thought that the stones were now his.

Finally he fell asleep. He tossed restlessly almost the entire night. Once he dreamed of the man he had known as Norris Haldorn.

In the morning, after Hymie Gold got up, old Mark Lewis came out to the *Johanna Jones*. Lewis was the sleek, silver-haired, senior United States Commissioner; a small, carefully-brushed man who wore rimless octagonal spectacles and gray suits of worsted. He talked with the expressionless voice of a shoe store salesman, but that merely disguised his cunning. Among the group that controlled federal politics, Old Man Lewis, as Hymie knew, had a considerable, if not actually a dominating, voice. At any rate, he fully controlled one important office—that of the legal advisor to the prohibition administrator. Jackson Fish, who held that job, was Lewis' son-in-law and had been tucked into the position by him. All warrants, for search or arrest, and every other document in the dry office, had to be passed upon first by Fish. To take care of friends was an easy, lucrative enterprise. One of these friends, customers really, was Hymie Gold.

When Lewis came up over the side of the boat, Hymie was surprised and pleased and somewhat worried. This was Lewis' first visit aboard the *Johanna Jones*. Why? Mark came over and sat down beside Hymie's wheel chair. The gray of his suit, the buff of his cheeks, and the silver of his hair, all blended into the soft blue Hymie could see behind him.

"What the hell did you do to a woman?" Mark Lewis seemed bored as he asked the question.

"All right, judge," Hymie said; "spill it."

"You must have done something to a woman. Something rotten. Whoever she is, she's put the treasury people hot on top of you and you've been indicted."

"The dirty bitch! Who is she?"

"This is no occasion for silly anger," Mark Lewis went on, stiffly. "I'm not concerned with your profanity. I don't know who the woman is. I came out here to warn you, for one thing, and to see if you could name this informer. She may still be betraying you. All I could find out was her sex. They won't tell me her name." After a minute he said, "It's a little sharp, this wind out here. I'd like a drink."

Hymie sent a boy for the drinks. "I know who the dame is," he said slowly. "It just come to me. Buddy Roberts' sister is who it is. Remember?"

Lewis said he didn't remember.

"Oh, he used to do a little bookkeeping for me and later on I let him go. Then somebody rubbed him out. His sister thinks it was me. Shorty must 'a' hung onto some of them books and give them to his sister and that's how she give the dope to the feds. But, Christ, *indicted!* You mean it's all voted already?"

"All voted," Mark nodded. "Hymie, I'm afraid you're in for it."

Hymie chuckled. It was a wholly senseless sound made only by his throat; he didn't know why he did it. He often made that sound when he couldn't think of anything to say. Accidentally, it had given him a reputation for nerve.

"You and me been good pals, ain't we, judge? It won't be much for you to handle."

"I'm not talking to you at all about that kind of business," Lewis announced curtly. He folded his hands across his chest and looked like a department store floorwalker. "The danger is too great."

"What danger?" Hymie demanded. "We ain't had no breaks for a long time."

"No danger—to you. You have nothing to lose. Absolutely nothing to lose by asking my help. And that goes no matter whether you offer a hundred thousand dollars or a hundred. I have nothing at all to gain and all to lose, and that's the only aspect I'm concerned with."

"You won't get no hundred grand, judge." Hymie felt, dimly, that he had been insulted. His manner shifted; the meaning of Lewis' words began to penetrate.

"You say I—me—I'm indicted by the federal grand jury?"

"On nineteen counts; violating the income tax laws and conspiring to violate internal revenue statutes," Lewis explained. "I would have sent someone else out here if it wasn't that I wanted to help you."

"You're a good guy," Hymie assured him. "How do we beat this business?"

"I'm more concerned with the matter I came out here for, primarily," Old Mark announced heavily. "I've brought out a bail bond, already signed, for thirty thousand. I think that will cover everything. When the deputy marshals get here, I'll release you. Then you won't have to go ashore. It isn't that you'd stay in a cell there very long, but those internal revenue boys would take you to a hotel room. They're clever and cold as steel. I don't like them. I should hate to think of them sticking it into you for three or four hours, with all they know already. I was thinking of your benefit when I came today."

"I guess I could get away for awhile. Maybe up to Vancouver. Let it blow over the way I done with them two county indictments," Hymie began. "That way, if—"

"Don't be a damned fool, Kid," Mark interrupted sharply. "What's the matter with you? You seem to be losing your grip. All around. I've noticed it for months."

"There's nothing wrong with me," Hymie told him angrily. He almost added, "You stinking yellow-belly."

"There most definitely is," Lewis insisted. He took another drink from the bottle on the tray, followed it with a full glass of water, and made a wry face. "If you drink a lot of your own liquor, and this stuff is a sample of what it's come to, I don't wonder you're changed." He wiped his short, narrow lips carefully with his handkerchief. "You talked about running away. You know that's as good as pleading guilty. And these indictments mean a real twenty years if you get the maximum. They're gunpowder under you. I mean it."

"Hell!" Hymie squirmed under his soiled blue lap robe. "You got to fix this up quick."

Mark Lewis sat back and peered coldly into Hymie's face. "You are losing your head, Gold, when you talk like that to me. We have done business, yes; but this is different. And conditions are different. I can't do a thing except release you on bond when you're arrested. I might be able to get you a few months' postponement, but that's all. This case goes right to the district court. I wouldn't have any say on it. And with Bandallo in the district attorney's office there's no way of quashing it. It would be murder to try. Just murder."

Old Man Lewis stretched his hand out of his sleeve and looked at his wrist watch. His forearm was thin, bony and brittle, of a sand color. "I wish they would get out here. I hate to be out of town so long. If the newspapers took on to what I'm doing for you it would be nasty. They would be devilish about it." He reached out and laid his hand on Hymie's thick forearm in what was palpably meant for a confidential, friendly pat as a prelude to a remark of special significance. "You know I'll be with you so long as you keep your mouth shut, Kid. You understand that if you talk—about things—then you'll harm me in such a way I won't be able to help you in any way. Just for your own good, I mean. It's all cooperative."

"What the hell, judge! Do I talk? I make my own fights," Hymie told him.

"Oh, I know that," Lewis assured him blandly. "I just wanted to point the thing out to you in the right light. For some reason that I can't understand, dark times have come upon all of us. Like a terrible blight. We have to be careful or we're all going to be smashed. It's strange, because if anything we have all taken fewer risks than usual. Isn't that true on your end?"

"My end will always be took care of by myself," Hymie proclaimed earnestly. "But what about your end of this, what I want to know, commissioner? See what I mean? Taking care of me on this here indictment."

Mark Lewis stared at him with eyes troubled and quizzical. "We'll have a big celebration if you get out of this one, Kid," he mused. "Quite an impressive party. You can take all the credit. You and your attorney, that is. I'll just sort of stand by and look on." Abruptly he was more direct, harsher: "I'll be looking on because there won't be any credit due me for getting you out. I can't be doing any ... business on this one. Don't sit there inviting me to take care of anything." He began to breathe heavily.

"You don't act like you used to—not as smart, Hymie.... Get your mind on this and get a lawyer busy."

The deputy marshals were meek at first, obviously cowed by the realization that they were miles at sea and actually aboard the notorious *Johanna Jones* about which they had read so much in the newspapers. Both of them were fat, their jobs were political, and it was not often that they were called upon to make an arrest like this, without police and other reinforcements.

Presently, reassured by the familiar presence of Commissioner Lewis, they grew bolder. Lewis took them away, finally, when they began to go poking through the gambling rooms, like a pair of curious children.

Hymie, left alone on deck, let his eyes rest on the green turbulence of the sea. He filled his lungs with cigar smoke. Did Lewis think he was so damned dumb? He knew what Lewis had meant; but he had had to make him believe that Hymie Gold might be dangerous, so that Lewis would exert every effort to extricate him from the web of those indictments. Hymie doubted his success. He suspected that Lewis would do no more than he had said. He had to plan something new, immediately. And he was on bad terms with his own lawyer; they had quarreled a year ago,—long enough for the man to have spread the story that Hymie Gold had refused to recognize his obligations to his legal help. That meant that he was probably on the blacklist of every useful lawyer, the kind he himself would choose. The other kind were either too dignified to meddle with shady clients or they were mere snorts, newly out of school, untried, dangerous.

A drove of Italian fishing boats was chugging and bobbing by about a half-mile east. Presently a great flock of sea-gulls came out to meet them to get the refuse the fishermen daily threw to them. The wind, coming out of the south, carried their forlorn, shrill calls to the *Johanna Jones*. A half-hour later, the wind had blown some clouds overhead. Those damned Italians were responsible for these bad times, Hymie said to himself as he watched the fishermen. They were fishermen now, all right, but soon they'd be running every still and every joint in the state. Foreigners should be kept out of the country, he muttered to himself; the country didn't need them.

The wind had increased in velocity. Now it began to blow wisps of cold spray into Hymie's face. Dexterously, he twisted his wheel chair, threw it forward upon its two small front wheels and worked it further into the corner so that the walls protected him. The problem began to clear as his cigar grew shorter. He decided, first, that he wasn't going to talk this over with any of the others; the less they knew about it the better. If they thought he was in a bad way, they'd probably desert him altogether.

What he had to do first, Hymie decided, was to get himself a good lawyer. He knew it would be easy enough to have the McDonoughs or the Fidelity or one of the other bonding people in his group get him one, but the kind he needed,—the shrewd, sharp, old ones with hidden connections of value,—that kind, he was sure, would have nothing to do with him. They hated him.

Hymie had been sitting in the lee of the cabin wing for an hour. He was growing cold. Suddenly, without preliminaries, a plan flashed on him. He hadn't been thinking of it at all, when the problem was miraculously solved. The solution dawned on him so mysteriously that he decided to use it. It was a hunch. When there was nothing else against them, hunches were always to be played. Now that he had something definite to work on, Hymie wanted to get going, to move physically. The deck was deserted. He slid down the wickerwork incline that extended from the seat of his wheel chair, and rolled himself along the deck silently. He used wooden blocks shaped like laundry irons, topped by silver handles, to propel himself.

The sheer cunning of his hunch aroused in Hymie a new and huge regard for his own mental gifts. The whole problem was easy now. Nothing to it. His man was to be Stoner Young, that attorney for the Haldorn outfit who had been with McMoyle on that dirty raid. From his anger at the raid he now excluded Stoner Young. Young must be a lawyer of gigantic ability. Even if he did talk as if his tongue were curled up on itself. Better, he thought, than any of these local bums. Bums was what they were. Young was an eastern man and hooked up with the most powerful interests in the country. The Haldorns were like the Rockefellers. To handle a case like this would be a cold cinch for Young. Just a cinch. And it would be easy to get him to take the case. You could tell that from his face,—it had a certain softness to it, as well as tolerance and humor. And Young had made it clear how anxious he was to learn what Hymie had heard, listening on the telephone to the last words of that Haldorn fellow.

Make a trade. Simple. "Listen, Mister Young; you want something from me and I'm willing to do business with you. You take my case and I pay you with the dope you want to know." He could see Young's face light up and he could hear him say, "Fine. In a week I'll have those indictments taken care of. Don't worry."

There was only one way to do it; that was to go ashore and see Young himself.

It was about ten P.M. when Hymie left the Haldorn residence in Hillsborough. He grinned with satisfaction as his two men lifted him down the stairs, into a warm, mellow California night. Matters were arranged. He need no longer worry, or even think about those indictments, Stoner Young had assured him. At the time, Hymie had been a little apprehensive of the curious, sad small smile upon Young's face, but now he put Young's smile down to friendliness. There had been no mockery in his voice. He was, Hymie felt sure, earnest and sincere in his promise to keep the pact they had made. Maybe Young was due for a shock when he heard what Hymie had to tell him about that telephone conversation. No, hardly a shock; more of a disappointment. Well, that was his business. The agreement was made. And if Young didn't like what he was told, once the indictments were dismissed, why he could just go to hell.

There was a short cement walk running off to the right at the foot of the steps, while straight ahead was the main driveway, laid in gravel. At the end of the sidewalk, behind a fringe of fronds, a fountain spouted. It would be pleasant, Hymie felt, to go and stay beside it for a while before starting the long drive back to the pier. He hated the drive. He would have to sit tensely, gripping straps on each side of the seat, and he would suffer acutely as he always did when driving. He rolled silently onto the concrete.

"You stand here and wait a while," he told the two men he had brought with him. Stand and wait was all they *could* do, Hymie reflected. What a bunch of no-goods! Taking his fat money and doing nothing to earn it. He shrugged that thought away and his mind began to brood on other unpleasant things: Jimmy Scrame, and that Devlin Kurtz fellow; that unfortunate *Malahat* deal; and the knifing in the Tampico Club, done at his order …

He rolled to the circle of trees edging the fountain and stopped. There was a woman at the fountain, with her back to him. Blue lights on the rim of the fountain basin sharply outlined her body under its white gown. She was silhouetted against the bright blue light as if she were nude. Hymie took the cigar from his mouth. With the smoke thinning in his nostrils, he began to smell heliotrope, a heavy scent rich with sweetness. His tongue wet his lips, and twice he had to swallow an excess of saliva.

Hymie stared at the legs of Night Haldorn. They were slim and lovely and he wanted them. Desire welled up in him like a storm at sea. He floundered helplessly. But it was not with lust that Hymie stared at those legs; it was with devotion and awe.

He pictured to himself, by way of contrast and with terrible completeness, his own humiliated body; a head, a chest, and a belly, strapped to a pair of glorified roller skates. He shuddered and closed his eyes, as though this were a nightmare, as though it were not true, while his eyes were still closed, he began to see again the superb legs of the woman.

He opened his eyes. The legs were no longer there. Night Haldorn had gone.

On the way back to Moss Beach, by limousine, Brats said: "Did you get a load of that gal in the garden? Boy, what a pip."

"A pip all right," Mealy said. "Know who that was? That's that Haldorn dame, Mrs. Norris Haldorn—" His voice assumed a ludicrous falsetto "—the young and beeyootiful widow. Boy, I'd like to have a go at her, all right. Boy."

"Boy," Brats agreed solemnly.

Hymie, from the back seat, shouted: "Close your dirty traps, God damn you! And keep them shut!" So that was the guy's widow. Well, he'd be bitched! So that was her, huh? *Mrs. Norris Haldorn* ...

"I seen her pitcher in the paper, in the Call," Mealy ventured. "She's got a kind of a goofy front name. Night. Night Haldorn. Ain't that the nuts?"

CHAPTER FOURTEEN

"FOUR HUNDRED BUCKS is no kind of money," Hymie complained. "Three hours in a cheap blackjack game for just four hundred measly dollars. Pfui!"

Royla said: "Why don't you kiss me, daddy?"

He did. Her thighs clung to his bare underbody, clung to the tender-skinned stumps, scarred and crimson. But he kept on thinking, angrily, of spending three hours to win four hundred dollars.

"Wasted my time," he grumbled again.

"Forget about it now, daddy," Royla soothed him.

"To hell with you," Hymie said. "I *want* to think about it." He sent Royla away and began to drink. Brandy. After a while his head drooped and he began to snore.

He dreamed that he was walking through a vast and stately palace, moving across dignified halls domed in blue. They seemed to be crowded with pillars. The floor felt warm against the soles of his feet. He had feet. And he passed into a place of arches and colonnades and was surrounded by clouds of white columns and shafts, shrouded in transparent gauze. All of these became white movement, swirling slowly, pressing toward him. They slowed. Stopped. And he saw that they had paired. Each pair was a replica of the legs he had seen that night in Hillsborough. When he awoke, crying harshly that he would go mad, he was covered with a cold sweat.

He lay there, obsessed by the thought of those limbs. Never had he wanted anything as fiercely as he wanted them now. Nothing else would do to still that strange hunger within him. He didn't want the woman; it wasn't sex he wanted, it was legs. As far as he was concerned, her bed need never be violated. He wanted her legs; to possess them, to look at them whenever he chose, to bask in the glow of their warm and lovely reality.

He twisted around on his bed. There, at the other end of the room, was the woman of the lovely legs. Hymie held his breath, for fear that breathing would dispel the illusion. She had her back to him, as before; but those legs, rising to those small buttocks, were unmistakable. Hymie took a breath, expecting the woman to vanish. She remained. Was he mad? He was crazy to believe that she was really in his bedroom.

Hauling himself to the edge of his couch, he pulled himself upright against the pillows and turned on more lamps. He gulped another tumbler of brandy. He tried not to see the legs. He forced his mind away from the image. He thought of the Antwerp deal and of Kurtz. He thought of Norris Haldorn, who was dead. When he looked up again he saw that the legs were still there. The woman seemed to have moved around to the foot of the bed. After rubbing his eyes furiously, Hymie looked across the room to the door. The legs were there, woman on top of them. Wherever he looked, there they were. When he moved forward on his sheets, they moved, too, as if he were looking at a photograph held by an invisible hand just within reach of his eyes. The legs were *with* him, no matter where he turned. Some one had switched his liquor. That was it. Bad alcohol was tricking his eyes. Fury rocked him. The bastard! To give Hymie Gold bum liquor. He pressed the bell that rang in Royla's bedroom and, while he waited, pushed back stiffly against the pillows. Sleepy-eyed, she came in dressed in a pair of mauve pajamas. The expression on his face awakened her.

"What's the matter? You sick, Hymie?"

"No. I ain't sick. Don't ask those lousy questions. Roll my legs over here."

"Sure, don't get mad." Royla looked puzzled and hurt. She boosted him up on the marble shanks and strapped him tight into place.

"Now roll me around the room," he ordered.

Royla suspected he was drunk. He didn't talk as if he was, though. She wondered if he had begun sniffing cocaine. At that, the glaze on his eyes looked more as if he had had a needleful of morphine. She kept pushing Hymie and his marble legs around the room. Hymie said nothing. Wherever he moved, or looked, or turned, there were the legs. It began to frighten him. Maybe it wasn't the liquor. Maybe he was mad.

Royla laid her hand on his forehead. "You better go to bed, Kid." Something had happened to her Hymie Gold. "You better go to bed," she repeated.

Hymie thought so too. Maybe, by morning, the thing would be gone. Perhaps the night would purge him of it. Royla unstrapped him. Confused, frightened, grateful, he lay with Royla.

Darkness helped to dispel the image of the legs; but his desire to possess them grew.

CHAPTER FIFTEEN

THE *Johanna Jones* drowsed in the strong sunlight of noon, tugging gently at her deep anchors. The water made a slopping sound against her sides. Her gaming rooms lay dusty and quiet. When a swell heaved her gently up, her old plates wheezed. She lay haggard and bleached, like an old harlot. Once a sleepy man lurched across her decks and disappeared. Nothing else moved.

But downstairs, turmoil seethed. Hymie Gold was drunk, furiously drunk. He rolled himself on his quilts in alternate paroxysms of terror and blind wanting, squeezing his lids tight shut to obliterate the vision, only to succumb each time to the overwhelming need for opening them again to see if it were still there.

In Royla's memory, he had never before been seized like this,—and her memory went back to many a weird revel. Still in lingerie, she bobbed rhythmically back and forth in a rocking-chair near the bed, watching. Hymie seemed to have gone mad ... mad with lust for another woman. For the first time in her life, Royla felt jealous. The sensation astonished her.

Hymie babbled. His lips slobbered. Sometimes he groaned, "O-oh Jee-zuz ... them legs!" And several times he called the names, "Oh, Norris Haldorn ... Night Haldorn." Royla seethed with anger. She had never denied Hymie Gold anything. Why should he go chasing now after another woman? Royla prodded him with questions. From what he told her, she gathered that Hymie lusted after a cold but beautiful woman who, apparently, wanted none of him. And she knew the bitter and dogged way he would carry on until he got what he wanted. She, Royla, might suffer a long time in that process. And it seemed to her that neither he nor she could return to the pleasant and ordered orgies of the past until this passion of his was stifled or satiated. So Royla came to a decision ...

She went into her own bedroom and curled up to read *True Story* until Hymie should sleep himself into sobriety.

"How you feel now, papa? Better?"

Hymie belched.

"There's something I want to talk to you about, daddy. You hear me? You awake?"

"Uh," Hymie croaked, his throat dry. The taste in his mouth angered him. He opened his mouth wide, as a chimpanzee does. "Bottom of a birdcage," he said harshly. He heard Royla's voice as if it came from the next room. He disliked closing his mouth when it tasted like that; a thumb went in and scraped around. He raised himself on one elbow. Thirst suddenly clawed at his tongue. He seized the pitcher beside his couch and drank greedily, in great gulps. Water drooled from the left corner of his mouth. After he set the pitcher down he fell back upon the pillows.

"I don't feel so good myself," Royla said. She slid her fingers over his palm and pressed them down. "Every once in a while I get sick of this ship. Ya know that, daddy?"

"Jeezuz, I'm sick," Hymie groaned.

"This sea gets me to rolling around inside and balls my insides all up," Royla proceeded, determined, calm.

"Jeezuz my insides are sick."

Royla understood what she was about. She went on firmly, "I got to get away from this boat for awhile or I'm gonna be good and sick." She watched him narrowly. Hymie turned his head and looked biliously at her. "Not feeling good, huh, baby?"

"Lousy, papa. The both of us got to get off of here for a while, see?"

Hymie belched again; he felt immensely relieved. "Hello, sunshine," he said, attempting brightness grotesquely. His tone implied he had just seen her.

"I said I feel sick and I got to get off of this God damned scow for a few days, daddy. We both need it."

"I can't get away right now," Hymie said. "Not right now. Business. Wait a while. Season'll be over in October anyhow."

"October!" Royla sniffed. *"October!"* Her nose shrugged. "To hell with October. I told you my insides was getting gummed up out here in this barge. We got to go ashore now."

"No!" he bellowed.

Royla pouted, "Aw. A-a-w."

"Cripes, go by yourself if you want to go." Cunning awoke. "Sure go, baby. You go ahead. Go for a couple of weeks."

"No; not by my lonesome."

"Yeah; you go on and go, baby."

Royla said loudly, *"No."*

"Don't tell *me* what you're gonna do. *You go!"* He had a terrifying, a fascinating, a terrible glimpse of those legs again. They melted. Hymie trembled. He repeated jerkily, "You—go."

"All right, if you want me to, then," Royla said meekly. She purred, inside, satisfied. This much had been arranged as she wished. Arising, she came over against the bed. Hymie dozed and blinked, and drowsed and jerked awake, and slid away again into leaden sleep. Under the quilts, Royla's fingers rubbed his naked loins. She congratulated herself on the success of her plan. She didn't intend to go ashore. She'd have to act warily, of course, to convince Hymie she was really leaving the ship. But she knew just how she could do that. And she had already selected her hiding place.

CHAPTER SIXTEEN

NIGHT HALDORN came out onto the porch and walked slowly to the far end, to a seat under a trellis of lilacs. A soft peace, the suspended quiet of dusk, lay pensively over the land. Night sat down and began fussing with her handkerchief. God, wasn't she *ever* going to be let alone? Wasn't she ever going to live her life as *she* wanted to live it? Wasn't there a day coming when she would be free? Her hand reached out, plucked a small branch of lilacs and brought it to her face. Was she not entitled to respect as the widow of Norris Haldorn, as the actual head of the great house of Haldorn?

To Lucia Gambier, her daughter's new dignity and power meant nothing. Night tensed, sitting very straight on the bench, stiff with bitter anger. The constant nagging and humiliation by her mother was horrible. It was as if a man, having succeeded to the command of an army going into battle, were to be pursued and anxiously lectured and admonished by a spinster aunt on the necessity for maintaining the moral fiber. She couldn't stand it. She wouldn't!

She took out the note that had come to her that afternoon and unfolded it. It was a strange note,—amusing or annoying, according to her mood,—and of itself almost meaningless. But as a symbol of her resentment against her mother's attitude, it had tremendous importance. Lilac petals floated down and rested softly on the back of her hand. She brushed them off and started to read. The note said:

"Baby, come out to the *Johanna Jones* at 11 o'clock to-night. I need to talk to you. The boat will leave the Moss Beach pier at 10:30."

It was typewritten and the name at the bottom of it, also type-written, was "Hymie Gold". The thing was meaningless. But it had been invested with ugly meaning when her mother had picked it up, read it and began to scold her. Night had answered: "Leave me alone, mother. I'm getting fed up on all this. I'm no longer a child, and I can take care of myself."

"Poppycock I"

"Well, say that if you want,—but I refuse to be dangling from apron-strings forever. Besides, and *incidentally*, I'm going to spend *my* fortune in my own way, without constant interference from you or anyone else."

"But you're all wrought up over nothing, child. I merely said ..."

"I don't care *what* you said. I'm not interested and I don't want to hear it. *Please* ..." And she raised her hand, in a gesture of annoyance, as though to stop her mother from talking fur-ther. When her mother, stunned for a moment by this outburst, seemed about to speak again, Night turned and rushed from the room.

Now she was under the trellis of lilacs rereading the note. Somewhere out beyond the dark lawn she could hear the shrill roar of a motor car as it sped over the gravel pathway. If her mother hadn't interfered she would probably have destroyed the note and forgotten about it. Now she had to see what it was all about—just to prove her independence. It was a silly note any-way—and undoubtedly it had been sent to her by mistake. But now that her mother had raised such a rumpus over it, she was bound to see it through, just for the devil of it. Anyhow, it would be amusing to go out to this ship. She seemed to remember having read about it. *The ship that never sailed ...*

Lucia Gambier's sharp voice splintered the darkness. "What are you up to out there, child?" Night didn't answer. "Come, you'll have to shake this nasty mood, Night. You'll only get to feeling worse if you stay out alone on a dark porch like this."

"I'll be getting up in a few minutes, but you may as well know now, I'm going out to that ship ... the one in the note."

"*Child!* You don't know what you're doing. You don't know what you're saying. You can't do that. What will people say?"

"You're wrong, mother. I'm not a child; I'm a widow. And not only can I do it, but I positively *will!* Moreover, I don't care at all what people will say."

"Please, child, don't keep that up. You don't know how silly it sounds to me. It isn't any credit to you, you know, because your husband was killed. And you might try to show me a little more respect when you talk to me. Come now, dear; we'll go inside. I want to talk to you ... something important."

"If it's anything you want me to sign," Night said wearily, "I won't. I won't do it, I tell you. I'm sick to death of living in an atmosphere that's rooted in the idea that being the widow of Norris Haldorn was the destiny I was born for. Why, you make a regular business of it. Mary Jones is a seamstress and Helen Smith was trained to be a singer and Anne Strong is a writer and you and I are widows. A profession. A living." She puffed at her cigarette, making its red head glow in the darkness.

"Don't take the idea of widowhood so seriously. You simply must relax and let things slide. I know what it is, dear. You're worrying about things. You mustn't, dear ... no."

"Oh, for God's sake, quit," Night groaned. "I'm not grieving about being a widow. Do you suppose I was sorry when—"

"Don't!" Mrs. Gambier broke in sharply. "Stop it! Here you are, with the whole world at your beck and call, saying things like that. Things that are just too contemptible." Lucia Gambier shook her head violently. Night jumped up and swept by her unseen. Mrs. Gambier continued to talk. Finally she had nothing more to say. She shook her head angrily. The whirr of an automobile starter grated on the air like a coarse file. Rubber tires in motion threw gravel against the fenders with a tinny rattle. A tail light shone like a red eye in the dark.

After a moment of silent exasperation, Mrs. Gambier was calm. She remembered, comfortably, that Night was after all *her* daughter. There was no cause to worry. The girl might be a little headstrong, but she couldn't be other than capable. Mrs. Gambier decided to say nothing more about the note or the ship.

CHAPTER SEVENTEEN

NORRIS waited for Kurtz to return. He strolled restlessly through the lobby, watching the gradual emergence of the Metropolitan Hotel from the hush that settles over it during the siesta hour at three in the afternoon. Clerks leaned sleepily over marble counters making idle marks on green blotters; others languidly answered telephone calls. People trickled through the doors and dripped reluctantly into the elevators. The starter clicked his signals sluggishly. Two men behind Norris argued wearily about a bridge hand, their voices the buzz of flies on a hot day. A fat man, asleep in a chair with an absurdly tall back, held a poodle lumped in his lap.

He ought, Norris thought, to feel tense, excited; he was strangely calm. He had met Devlin Kurtz an hour ago. Norris was standing at the counter of a street-corner orange-juice stand. A thin hand suddenly clutched his arm from behind, and a voice with a nasal twang said:

"Ah, M'sieu Blackburn …"

Norris pretended to wipe perspiration from his face with his handkerchief as he turned slowly around.

"My face was badly cut up. Airplane accident," he explained before showing Kurtz the gnarled, purple cheeks under the handkerchief. Kurtz whistled sharply between his teeth, but there was no surprise in his eyes.

"It is your back what h-tell me you are h-Eddie h-Blackburn," Kurtz told Norris. His eyes protruded slightly and there was a lump on his neck which Norris recognized as a form of goitre. "If I see your h-face first I h-say h-this is not my h-frien'. Even your eyes are h-change. And your h-voice, it sound h-like you got blotter in your h-mouth. What have happen' to h-you?"

He stood shorter by a foot than Norris; and he wore a hairy fedora with an uncreased crown in the French fashion, pulled low to his ears. This, even with the tendency to raise his shoulders, didn't mark him a Jew. He was, Norris learned later, a Roumanian, a lawyer.

"Right h-now I am oh so h-glad to see you; I give you my h-word. I cancel my bill, so. Like that. You owe me h-nothing." He spread his palms and smiled and his large, fuzzy eyebrows, like plump caterpillars squirming over his nose, almost hid his eyes. "This shall be h-five h-thousand dollar' I am give you, my frien'. Five h-thousand I tell you h-right, too. I get this charge h-dismiss'. I get him h-quashed."

To every verb, as Devlin Kurtz spoke, he gave special emphasis, a pat on the head; this gave a sing-song, chanting quality to his conversation. Norris was grateful that the fellow had chosen to talk; it gave him time in which to adjust himself to this new situation. He wondered why Kurtz was so glad to see Blackburn.

"Tit for h-tat, eh?" Kurtz was smirking. "You for me and h-me for you, eh?"

"Come out of this," Norris said sharply. "I won't talk to you here."

Kurtz nodded understandingly. "In an hour I h-see you in my rooms at the Mark Hopkins." He pressed a card into Norris' hand, squeezed his forearm again and walked away.

This must have been one of the old hangouts of Ed Blackburn. Norris felt a chill come over him as he remembered that he was impersonating a dead man,—one who had been murdered mysteriously. Had Night's husband been shot as Blackburn or as Haldorn? And what would the murderer do if he discovered he had killed the wrong man? Norris shuddered at the thought.

Devlin Kurtz walked into the lobby, spotted Norris, and came over to him. They went up in the elevator, to the seventeenth floor. While Norris waited for Kurtz to find the key and open the door, he tried to get clear in his mind the advantages, if any, of the course he was following. It was dangerous, of course. But he had to continue these efforts to reach the truth in the case, or abandon everything and become reconciled to using a false name, Stoner Young or some other, the rest of his life. Once in the room, Kurtz expanded his affable manner in spite of Norris' deliberate curtness. Kurtz rested his elbows on the arms of his chair, interlaced his fingers, and began, "I h-think you have one h-grand guts to come back here. One h-very grand guts." He talked fast and the extra nose tones he prefixed to his words slurred into a curious accompaniment that sounded like, *"hon-hon-hon-hon."* He went on, "H-maybe you are smarter than h-that. I do not recognize you, h-no, not if 1 see you h-from the h-front. Your face have a h-different h-set. You h-talk funny, so I could h-think you have sore h-throat. Ah, am gottam h-glad to h-see you, Eddie." They were both silent for a few seconds, then Kurtz spoke again, "We have h-some h-li'l h-business together I think, too. Our frien' on the boat he is still h-rolling aroun' you h-know."

Apparently, Kurtz was trying to trap him. At first Norris merely nodded, then, as an afterthought, he ventured, "A neat job, a neat job." The phrase had occurred to him as characteristic of Blackburn. It seemed to please Kurtz.

"Oh, non, that was not h-neat—non, but very h-bloody. Oh, it was h-so very good to h-see it. Why be neat," he shrugged, "with dogs! When we h-stick pigs we h-like to see the blood h-gush. You took care of one h-Gold. A h-pig is always a pig. For that h-little job I am always h-glad to do somethin' to repay you. You h-give Hymie's h-brother a li'l h-ticket." With ludicrous concern lest his trousers be rumpled, he crossed his knees. When this tender operation was completed he looked up. Norris was grinning.

"What you h-laugh at, eh?" Kurtz demanded. "You h-think of sometheen' maybe? Well, there is not the necessity. I have h-already do the thinking, my frien'. You have your reasons to hate this h-bastard an' I have my h-reasons. And you have h-no more to be afraid of. You see? You have h-new face. An' I have h-this charge dismissed. The h-law do not want you any more. I have h-fix this for h-you. But this bastard, h-Gold, he would like to cut h-your heart out and h-mine, too, I tell you."

Norris said, "What's between you and Hymie, Kurtz?" And then, as he saw perplexity whirl across Kurtz's face, he added, "The same old trouble, I guess, eh?"

Kurtz asked, with shrewd carelessness, "How h-does your head h-feel, Eddie? She was hurt in this h-crash also?" Norris smiling, guessed: "Oh, you mean the ship."

Devlin Kurtz unbent to his feet and began to pace the room with quick steps. "H-yes, yes, h-that an' all that. I am too h-quick. Perhaps h-you forget when you have been away. You have been so h-long away. Never answer h-my last h-letter, do you? Now you tell me h-truly—no, you do not h-remember." Norris said, "No, I don't remember the exact circumstances. I was in the hospital, unconscious for months."

There was an expression almost sympathetic in Kurtz's face now. He shook his head violently, as a mark of sorrow, and then he began to speak again. "You h-will recall the *Favala?* The one

I buy in h-Antwerp. Oh, h-what a cargo, my frien'. Ho-oh God, h-what a cargo she take. I put seventy h-thousand dollars in that h-cargo. I am to mak' two hundred thousand when h-she get here to this h-side. Everything I h-arrange." His gesture became more and more emphatic. "An' who highjacks h-that h-boat? Who high-jacks h-that h-boat when she h-come to the Farallones, eh? Who h-does that? You h-know who do h-that. Dirty h-putrid bastard Hymie h-Gold. And h-sink my ship, too, I h-tell you." His throat was dry now; he poured himself a glass of heavy wine. As he drank, the white goitrous knots on his throat bobbed up and down.

Kurtz nervously paced the room again. It was oppressive, full of furniture. Chinese screens of imperial yellow hid two of the corners. Chairs and tables of various heights, all a gleaming black, one of them carved, stood about in disorder. An exquisite pair of blue Ming vases rested on taborets. A chaise-longue laden with silk cushions almost filled one corner.

"You h-must be in love when you h-sit like that and stare. You do not hear h-me," Kurtz said, but not unpleasantly. "No, you h-never know how to love a woman, Eddie. H-no. To love h-badly is one great h-mistake."

Grotesque as Norris considered this conversation to be, he nevertheless saw wisdom in keeping it going. It was possible that through this man Kurtz he might stumble on the whole strange truth about Blackburn and his murder, thereby achieving some success in the struggle to regain his name. To sue openly, he now knew, would not only be useless, but might even prove fatal. He fell in with Kurtz's conversation.

"A mistake? No, I think not. To love badly is a gift since it assures success in all other things. One does not occupy himself with women once he realizes his shortcomings."

"But h-you never h-know h-what it is to possess a h-woman completely," Kurtz replied, staring hard at Norris.

"And what of that? Suppose you take a flower and press it tightly in your fist. You've killed it; crushed it. That's your complete possession. But hold the flower gently, brush it with your lips softly,—that's better."

"Now," Kurtz said, "h-you have made a poet's h-description of a whore. One hundred h-men can brush their lips on your flower but h-only one can crush it. Yes, a whore. An' what do this Hymie Gold do to h-the woman I h-love? She is h-fresh and h-sweet like the summer h-peach and he h-take her. An' he made a bitch." Kurtz clenched his right fist fiercely and raised it. Norris interrupted.

"Come down to earth, Kurtz, what did you want to talk to me about?"

Wide, thin hands curled tensely on the black knobs of the chair arms and Kurtz said, "There h-is a h-way to get rid of this man—one h-good way with h-no trouble. You know h-what I like to do?"

"No, and I'm not sure I care."

"You h-don't know? I h-like to have this fellow tied up and I h-will come an' cut his stinking heart out with a dull knife. What h-you think of that?"

"Come out of it," Norris said coldly.

"I tell you what h-right now, Blackburn. We make a pact, eh—? God damn, what? Make a h-pact to h-kill this pig-son-of-a-pig. He is going to h-kill you first if he know you are back. You do not forget what he do to you at El Cerrito, hah? So, h-you got to do it. An' I h-got to do it. I tell why I got to—"

"Never mind that," Norris cut in. "Go on with your proposition." He was weary of Kurtz's emotional gymnastics.

"You have the h-nerve to kill Hymie Gold?"

"Sure, I have the nerve all right." Did Kurtz expect him to commit a murder? He'd have nothing to do with it. But he'd better find out what Kurtz had on his mind.

Kurtz moved hurriedly, changing his clothes. "We have to h-reconnoiter tonight, my frien'. Tonight we h-do this an' when we come back I h-tell you the whole plan. All h-very nice. Very simple. She will h-not be too hard for you. I will show you h-everything. I will h-tell you. We work this h-together, God damn, what?" He spoke gleefully now. "You an' me, we h-going out to this boat. We h-set the table, hah?"

CHAPTER EIGHTEEN

C UPPED in the soft upholstery of the limousine, Devlin
Kurtz's shoulders had risen to make a kind of sheath into
which he put his head by letting his neck go limp. He sat like that,
with hardly a word, through the whole ride. He seemed to have
bottled and capped himself so that some kind of fermentation
might proceed inside him.

He had insisted, after dinner, on an immediate start. Norris, after
protesting with assumed anger that the whole plan be revealed
to him at once, agreed. Norris felt that it didn't really matter
because all things were inevitably converging to a oneness that
would shortly be made manifest. That he himself had no hand
in actually precipitating this climax, he realized fully; he, as the
others, moved with events, but did not make them.

Kurtz puffed at a cigar. The car smelled of suspended tobacco
smoke. Norris wound down a window. The wind brought in the
cold, moist odors of clover and wild alfalfa, and later, the deep
odors of fresh-turned furrows.

The limousine lurched violently to the right and plunged into
a long dark tunnel of trees. The aromatic scent of the fields became
the sharp, salt air of ocean spray. Norris thought of Richard Todd
and of how his death had sent Norris into this weird adventure. If
only Richard were here to share it with him.

The car swerved again, into a narrower road going south. The pleasant San Mateo valley spread out on both sides. To the right loomed a shadow that grew suddenly huge as they approached it. As the car swept past, Norris dimly saw an old house with ornate gables and cupolas and a roof fenced by lightning rods.

They were going west again, along a paved road. The car sped over a rise and dipped down to a desolate gasoline station. The limousine stopped. About a hundred yards west lay the sand of the beach which stretched down to the breakers. A hooded lamp, like the candle-lit face of a cowled Franciscan, marked the beginning of the pier. A small boat was tied there, lifting and falling on the water.

Kurtz emerged from his lethargy and stepped from the car, stiff-legged and cramped. "Park here and wait for us," he told the chauffeur. He walked down the beach with Norris. Their shoes made weird noises in the sand.

"You h-will keep your face to the h-front so nobody h-will h-know you. Your back h-could give h-you away."

Norris said, "How about you?"

"Hymie Gold will h-not think to harm me," Kurtz replied stolidly. "Not on his own boat, my frien' … and h-not without some plan. He don't know I hate him h-because I tell no one … I h-keep anger to myself. Tonight at the h-gambling tables, I have eye on Hymie. Meantime h-you will be h-going h-'roun' to see where this bastard sleep at night. You will find out everythin' so you h-could go in the dark h-to his bed when you come again."

Norris nodded, saying nothing. After a short silence Kurtz began to chuckle to himself. In answer to the questioning look in Norris' face, Kurtz said,

"Very nice, I h-think, some night, to h-cut the cables. Wait for the good h-strong storm and cut the h-lines and there will be h-no more of this Hymie Gold."

They had reached the pier. Norris turned and looked back. The shore lay smooth and dark and empty as a sea horizon, except for the dull blue lights of the gasoline station.

They clambered down to the boat. Now that they were aboard, they saw that she was much longer than she had appeared from the beach.

A bench, upon which were scattered a dozen limp oilcloth cushions, hemmed the narrow stern and here they settled themselves for the ride to the *Johanna Jones*. The sound made by the sea as it slapped against the pier seemed pleasant to Norris. He looked back at the beach. A great motor bus, like an illuminated showcase, moved leisurely by and disappeared behind a hill. Devlin Kurtz, sitting beside him, began to crunch hard candy. He would stop chewing every so often to take the sweet pulp between his front teeth and suck on it noisily. Norris began to regret that he had come. He hoped that the roar of the motor would drown out this infuriating sound.

Automobile headlights flashed from shore and were suddenly darkened. Other cars had parked at the pier. In a little while, a chattering group of young people smelling of gin and cheap perfume, tumbled from the pier into the boat, and the pilot, after counting eleven on board, started the motor.

"Ay! *Hey!* Wait a while. There's more of our crowd coming yet. Ted and Alice and Fleta ain't here." A gangling fellow stood up and peered blearily around. A hand yanked him down. "Sure they are. Here's Alice in my lap."

They laughed.

A fine mist sprayed over the boat as it was bumped by waves. Norris hunted for a dry spot to scratch a match for his cigarette. But seat and gunwale and ribs were moist. The soles of his shoes were damp. Where the ribs on the side of the boat met the seat, there were corners, and Norris tried each of these within reach.

He spoiled four matches. He stood up, away from the seat, and lifted up the cushions and scratched the match quickly on the small disc of dry wood exposed. As he lifted the flaring stick and cupped it in his hands, a triangle of white paper caught his eye. The match blew out. He found, on searching his pockets, a box of matches with a sandpaper strip on the side. When the cigarette was going, he reached for the paper, and, walking to the cabin, read the words on the outside: "Mrs. Norris Haldorn." He unfolded the slip of paper and read the note Royla had written.

No realization, no understanding came, even after he had read the note several times. He knew, superficially, that the note told Night Gambier to come to Hymie Gold. But why? What was there between them?

The note definitely established the fact that there was some connection between lovely, desirable Night Gambier and Hymie Gold. What was it? Hymie hated Blackburn; did this link Night Gambier to the murder of Blackburn? Was it possible that Night had deliberately murdered Blackburn for the single purpose of obtaining control of the Haldorn-Empire fortune? Did this mean that Night had discovered Ed Blackburn was an impostor? Or was it Hymie who instigated the murder, persuading Night to be a party to it in exchange for control of Haldorn's estate, as a means of ridding himself of Blackburn?

Norris glanced at the radium dial of his wrist watch. The time was eleven thirty.

CHAPTER NINETEEN

BLACK-LACQUERED tray balanced on his hand, Teddy rapped on the door. Sandwiches, ginger ale and two whiskey highballs were on the tray. The door opened, throwing a weird yellow light on Teddy's immobile face. He peered inside. The room was one of many cabins which Hymie had outfitted in violet plush and mahogany for parties.

Teddy stepped inside and looked around. Royla was pressed flat against the door. "Quick," she said, "tell me. Did she come?" Her eyes ran over Teddy's black face, as if they were fingers feeling its satin darkness.

Teddy exhaled lengthily. It was momentous news he carried, and he wanted to savor the full flavor of it.

"Ya-as, *ma'am*. Sho' did come. Sho' did come awright."

"How do you know?" she glared. Teddy stepped back. "How do you know?"

"Why ... why ... why becawze Ah seen her go along of him into his room. Downstairs. That there room, Ah mean." His gaze wandered to the highballs, on the table now, and back again. "You ain' goin' do nothin' awful,—please?" Teddy trembled at the thought of the punishment that would crash over him should Hymie Gold discover his disloyalty through some act or word of Royla's.

"No. No, no; of course not, Ted."

"Ah think you got Hymie down aw wrong. Got him down aw wrong, now. Actually, you has. 'Sides, that gal ain' so swell lookin'. Hymie just got a li'l business with her. She ain' good lookin'. Nothin' like what you is." This was his honest opinion. Royla dazzled him. "She just a pert lookin' kid," scornfully. "Just a kid, not a real honest-to-God woman."

Fury seized Royla. Hymie thought she was ashore. Hymie had another woman in his room. Hymie was giving money to another woman. Hymie was giving her a diamond wrist watch, a ring, a necklace, greenbacks. If Hymie was killed, she would get his money. Hymie was giving her an automobile. Hymie was giving her a mink coat, fox furs, opening charge accounts for her at the stores.

"How long ago did she go with him?"

"Not long. Not long at all," Teddy assured her. "Just about a hour."

"*An hour!*" she almost screamed the words. "Why didn't you tell me before?"

"Ah couldn't get away."

"Did you see her come in?"

"How could Ah see her come in when Ah didn't know what her looked like at all until Hymie comes up to her and talks to her and says her name and everything."

"*He* came up to *her!*"

"Ya-as. He come right up to her all surprised-like."

"How old is she?"

"Oh … Well … 'Bout eighteen-nineteen somewhere."

Royla seemed to have forgotten that it was her note that had brought Night to the *Johanna Jones.* Only one thing concerned her now,—her future. She realized that she was in acute danger of being thrown back upon a hard world, and a hard life,—and she was close to thirty. What a fat chance she'd have of getting a job in a show now! And here, when she thought she was fixed with

Hymie, along comes this woman. A woman, moreover, who has money of her own.

Teddy said, "You want something more of me, ma'am?"

Royla gave him a five dollar bill. He pocketed it and let himself out furtively. She saw that he had taken the whiskey highballs and the sandwiches away with him.

Coming out of the passageway, Teddy saw Hymie sitting in his wheelchair. A waiter leaving a cabin with food still on his tray had, for Hymie, but one meaning: The waiter had happened upon an argument in a private room and had left the people to row it out among themselves. Hymie disliked arguments of that sort on his boat. Too often they led to guns. Tonight, especially, he did not want any fighting aboard the *Johanna Jones*.

Hymie called out. Teddy was too scared to lie. He told Hymie the number of the room. Then he hurried away, drank the highballs and a slug of gin from his own bottle, wrapped his white coat in a sheet of newspaper, put on his best clothes, and slid into the next boat leaving for shore. The job wasn't worth anything to him any more. He had thirty-one dollars in his pocket.

On the way back from the *Johanna Jones*, the speed boat passed a tug. With lazy curiosity, the pilot wondered what business a tug could pick up out here tonight. She was not moving ... semed to be waiting for something or some one.

It was a long time before Hymie started down the corridor. He had seen those limbs again ... seen them in the flesh. A magnificent sight blended of passion and pain; the fury of desire and the ache of loss.

Clouds hid the moon from the sea. The *Johanna Jones* tugged at her permanent anchors, heaving and rolling with the wind.

CHAPTER TWENTY

A HALF hour after they had come, Kurtz had consumed all of his whiskey. He had brought a flask with him. Bottled bravery, Norris thought to himself; without it Kurtz would have had little of his sham bravado.

"A little h-drink it sharpen the h-mind," Kurtz told Norris blandly. He turned his back to the bar and hooked a heel over the rail.

There was something wrong with the electric lights; the globes shone with a weak, yellow glow instead of with their usual brilliance. Kurtz, looking around for Hymie, saw thick angular pillars covered with mirrors, and a small dance floor overhung by a slowly revolving ball plastered with sharp fragments of glass that scintillated as it revolved. Hymie was not in sight.

"How you h-like the place?" Kurtz asked carelessly.

Norris nodded as he glanced about, but said nothing.

About twenty-five guests were scattered around the tables. Two of them, negroes, were escorting white women. The others accepted them with unconcern. Norris was shocked. One of the women was obviously a harlot, but the other was young and blonde and lovely to look at. If she were neurotic, it didn't show in her face. Norris saw her slide a small pink hand over the negro's dark one as it lay on the green cloth of the table. He turned away.

Two dice games merged suddenly amid a rattle of yells, and the hoarse crying of a stout woman in a green dress shattered the somber quiet that followed.

Norris had satisfied himself that Night was not in the room. He turned to Devlin Kurtz whose caution seemed to be ebbing.

"No h-one on the coast can overcome the syndicate I represent," Kurtz assured Norris solemnly. "But sometime h-members get pig-headed ideas about the law." He repeated this with emphasis, as though he had been contradicted. "Always the fools afraid to use force when it require. Always the h-God damn' injunction. That is not the h-way you have to h-choke the weeds in a flower garden. To h-kill off the weeds you need a hoe h-with a sharp edge an' you h-chop up the root'. Chop 'em up. H-got to chop 'em up. That is right. I say that is right!" He leaned over and seized the lapels of the bartender's limp and soiled white coat.

The fellow had a swollen under lip, and he must have been tired. He threw Kurtz off violently and cursed him. Norris, watching with increasing distaste, shook Kurtz by the shoulder.

"Damn it, brace up," he commanded savagely. He was no longer concerned with what Kurtz had in his mind. The thing that interested him now was the drama between Night Haldorn and the incredible Hymie. Devlin Kurtz was peering at him under his fierce, bushy eyebrows. With clumsy, deliberate motions and without shifting his eyes, he drew another flask from somewhere in his clothes and put its mouth to his lips. He took a long drink and gravely replaced the bottle. Norris turned his back to him.

A dull thud, at his feet, interrupted Norris' revery. Kurtz had fallen to the floor and was attempting, angrily and ludicrously, to get to his feet. Norris did not offer him a hand.

Night Haldorn came into the room. She wore a low-cut gown of shimmering black satin, and a jacket of white velvet. Her skirt touched the floor. The heels of her black moire slippers ticked audibly across the room.

At the top of the gown, where her breasts began to show, Night wore something that glowed. Norris thought he recognized it. No, it was impossible. How could she be wearing it? He watched, almost breathlessly, as she pressed through the group around the roulette table, and then he saw that he had not been mistaken.

She was wearing between her breasts the magnificent cluster of diamond and ruby set in gold which Narapatee had shown to him in the little Irrawaddy temple of the reclining Gaudama in Burma. He stared at it, transfixed. By what strange circumstance had Night acquired possession of the jewels? How did she come to be wearing on *her* breast this precious emblem of a lovely idyll in *his* life? He thought of those, soft, dreamful months with Narapatee. He realized how dear to him had become the memory of those tender days and languorous, passionate nights. He realized, too, that deep down within him, the affection he had had for Narapatee had slowly, wonderfully blossomed. He knew now, as he had never known before, what it meant to love another human being. Joy surged through him with the assurance that he was going back to Burma as soon as his affairs were in order.

Night was still gambling. Her face was flushed and nervous laughter quivered across her lips. She was winning, Norris saw. Not many were left at her table now. The dice game had broken up. There remained in the main salon only the five around the roulette table, a pair of sleepy waiters, Norris, the bartender, and Devlin Kurtz slumped in a stupor against the bar.

As Norris watched, Night won again. She threw back her head and laughed, almost hysterically. The motion of her shoulders drew back the white jacket, caught above her waist with a bow, and moved the jewels forward.

"Oh, glorious!" she cried out. "I love to win!"

She saw herself in the mirror on the pillar behind the croupier. She was proud of the strength she had discovered within herself. She had tested this strength in so many ways in the last few hours; she was amazed at her own fortitude.

Her coming here in the first place was a triumphant bursting of shackling chains; her mother had put up terrific resistance. Meeting Hymie Gold; that, too, had required courage. But a fearlessness, a gay daring greater than these, greater even than her passion for life, was in her acceptance of the jewels Hymie Gold had offered to her in his fat, limp hand.

She was glad now that she had taken the jewels. Hymie Gold had given them to her as a token of his inarticulate appreciation. Why shouldn't she have taken them? If she hadn't, some other woman would have. And besides, it was small enough payment for the horror of Hymie's presence. He had stared at her legs, and the way of his staring had been lewd and hard. With chill disgust she recalled that silent survey of Hymie's.

She moved around the table. The man next to her had reminded her of Hymie. She noticed, casually, that a disturbance had begun across the room.

Kurtz had inexplicably found the strength to stand up and begin drinking again. He had lurched violently against Norris. His first reaction was to snatch a thick plate from the counter and hurl it at the tired bartender. It struck the barkeep in the chest. Grunting with pain, he rushed at Kurtz, stretched over the counter, and smashed a slender green bottle across Kurtz's mouth. Blood appeared at once. The barkeep lifted the bottle and hit Kurtz again, this time on the forehead.

Rubbing his chest, the barkeep opened a gate in his counter and came out to where Devlin Kurtz lay on the floor. He lifted Kurtz by the armpits and dragged him behind the bar where he let him drop. He then spread a square of black oilcloth over the flat figure. A soiled white napkin clung to the oilcloth, where it covered Kurtz's chest and head.

"That," the barkeep explained to Norris, "is so you'll know where he is when you come to drag him home, the bum. And that better be quick, from the feel of this weather. Me, I'm leaving now."

Norris considered what to do. He felt no responsibility for Kurtz. Through the up-ended section of the counter, he could see the long, dark, shiny lump with the white marker. Kurtz didn't move.

After a while the bartender came out in his shirtsleeves, carrying his coat and a green ulster over his arm; he proceeded onto the deck.

Night was quarreling with someone at her table. She spoke quickly, emphasizing her remarks with angry gestures. The jewels, suspended between the two gentle hillocks of her breasts, flashed with every gesture. Norris watched without moving.

He saw her whirl around, cross the room with quick short steps, and stalk furiously through the doorway. The startled eyes of the players and the pallid eyes of the croupier followed her lithe body under the shimmering black gown until it disappeared from view. They turned back to their game. Norris hesitated a moment and then followed her through the doorway.

CHAPTER TWENTY-ONE

NORRIS stepped from the mellow warmth of the salon into a harsh, cold wind that whipped across the deck carrying sea spray with it. This savage intimacy with wind and water exhilarated Norris; he found it invigorating, tonic.

The wind bore down out of the northwest. Norris followed Night around the deck to the sea side. She faced the wind, bracing herself against its fierceness exultantly. She found in the brutal turbulence of wind and water a material counterpart for the emotional violence seething in her. Chaos inside clamored for chaos outside; there was tremendous satisfaction in matching the one with the other.

For the first time, defiance of her mother had found consummation in action. The result was gratifying. Of course her mother had been wrong. Her mother had always been wrong. This was the only way to live. Unless one lived bravely, acted with courage, one might just as well be dead. Her mother knew nothing about such things because she was afraid ... afraid for herself and afraid for others.

Holding her face up to the dark sky, feeling the moist wind kissing her throat, Night felt that she was free at last. The wind's kiss was a release and a promise. She felt glad.

A thin spear of light from the deck window fell upon Night. Seeing that tall, lovely body as the wind whipped the black gown around her, Norris realized how fortunate he was that his interest in women, physically, was so slight. His passions had been well in control. And even in his feeling for Narapatee there was more of bodyless spirit than of flesh. They had been as two who searched far, arm-in-arm, for joy of a quiet kind—this, rather than as man and woman who agonized in relief of lust. Had he been of another temper he might have developed a fatal desire for Night; fatal in that it would have checked him from upsetting her mastery of the Haldorn name and fortune. It gave Norris a certain grim satisfaction to see how lovely she looked; it would make more appropriate the eventual punishment he planned to visit upon her, render her dethronement exceptionally spectacular.

They stood on the seaward side of the *Johanna Jones*. On the land side, the last boat departed carrying a group of tense, frightened guests and gamblers.

Aboard the *Johanna Jones* there was no regular crew of seamen. She carried registration papers and clearance from Mazatlan. When she had last cleared that slatternly harbor she had carried as master one Orizon de Miranda, *capitan de marina*, Mexican navy, as well as a small crew. But Miranda and the crew had long since been sent ashore.

One of the gamblers suddenly remembered Night and realized she must still be aboard the ship, but when he shouted, the driver of the launch slapped a dirty hand across his face and shoved him violently back.

"Goddam fool!" The driver grunted. He pulled his starter back. "Goddam fool! Lucky if we get back as it is without screwin' around here any longer over some lousy wench." One of the croupiers pressed forward.

"Here, you can't act like that," he said sharply; "that man's a guest." The little boat fell away sickeningly and then jumped high and the croupier staggered and threw out his arms.

"You go to hell," the driver said. "Go to hell and shut your trap."

After that nobody spoke again about waiting. The driver continued muttering to himself. He wasn't any stinking deep water sailor, and if he got in safe this time he'd stick to the Suisun and the Sacramento run. His racket was produce trucking in the delta, he mumbled, and he had always hated this deep-sea taxi driving anyway.

Terror clutched at this fresh-water sailor. Monstrous black seas pushed shoulders under the boat, lifting it high and free. The boat rested high for a suspended second and then it dropped with a sickening rush. The odor of burning oil and the sharp hot smoke from the engine filled the little cabin, but they all stayed there and coughed and sweated and listened in fear to the jangling and racking of the motor. One of the men, noticing beads of sweat on the blue side of the engine, reached out with his handkerchief to wipe them off. The driver roared at him and he dropped his handkerchief as he drew back, shaking.

The noise of the engine drowned out the wheeze of the wind and the bursting shatter of water. The windows of the cabin were grimy with moisture. The passengers pressed dumbly against each other and stared at the boatman who hovered over his pounding cylinders.

When the driver looked up he saw the tug again. It had veered around and was now hard on the stern of the *Johanna Jones*. None of the frightened passengers saw the boat or the light. Two dim figures holding a blazing blue-tipped rod in their hands were apparently at work with an acetylene torch slicing through the anchor lines of the old gambling ship. The driver knew at once what was going on. "Jeeze," he said to himself, "they picked a swell night to cut them lines...." The rival syndicate was doing what it had so often threatened to do: it was destroying Hymie Gold's place of business.

Drenched, soggy with perspiration, the people in the cabin faced tensely forward, peering out to where they thought the shore ought to be. No one ventured outside though the hot and fetid air of the cabin made breathing difficult. There were dreadful moments when the propeller was out of the water and the boat shuddered helplessly.

The driver looked back at the old *Johanna Jones*. Her anchor line severed, she was no longer a pleasure resort but a ship furiously blown across a wild plateau of windswept water.

CHAPTER TWENTY-TWO

S HUT up, you old sow!" Hymie was surprised by the dry croaking sound of his voice. It made him angry. Royla was responsible. Royla was screaming at him. What right had she to be here anyhow? He wanted her to go away so he could look at the screen. The legs were there. As Royla screamed, the legs wavered and disappeared. He wanted them back. He knew they weren't the real ones. He was going to have the real ones later. Why was she screaming? Why didn't she go away? He wanted her to go away. He only wanted the legs. He saw her angry face close to his. He held his gun in his lap. Why should he let this sow yell into his face? He put his arm around her neck and her screaming stopped. That was nice. No more yelling.

He squeezed. She was going to cry. She did cry. He pulled her face a little lower. He raised the butt of his gun and swung it hard against her head. That made an ugly sound. It reminded him of the moist crunching when he had lost his own legs. She stiffened and jerked in his arm and a scream started deep down somewhere but couldn't get out. Now she was lying asleep across his wheel chair. He felt better. She wasn't going to shriek any more. He liked her that way when she was quiet.

Hymie Gold pushed Royla's limp body off his chair and it fell, face down, to the floor.

But the room was not quiet. A voice was still shouting.

"Anybody else want some of the same medicine? I'm the big shot around here and I get what I want."

He realized, mistily, that it was his own voice. The words fitted feelings inside him.

The ship listed heavily, dropped back, and then tugged still more violently. Hymie was thrown half out of his chair. The old hulk fell back on her keel and threw herself to the other side. Farther and farther she rolled. She broke her last line herself; she came free, shot back to starboard, and moved abruptly forward. Hymie's chair rolled on its side and spilled him to the floor.

He was holding on to the revolver. The lights went out.

Hymie rolled and bumped back and forth across the floor of the cabin as the *Johanna Jones* lurched dizzily up one side of each wave, only to plunge madly down the other. In the darkness, Royla came back to consciousness.

There were four people aboard the old boat, all drunk. Hymie Gold was drunk with insane lust. Night Gambier was drunk on new discovered power. Royla was drunk with mad wrath. Norris Haldorn was drunk with dark dreams. Four drunks aboard a drunken boat floundering about on a wind-torn sea.

CHAPTER TWENTY-THREE

L IGHTNING tore across the loud sky, revealing a woman's figure clinging to the rail of the *Johanna Jones*. Her dress flapped like a flag in the wind. She stared, enchanted, at the jagged streaks of light playing above the moving ship. Behind her, a cabin door banged open and shut with each staggering lurch of the vessel. Thunder rumbled and boomed overhead.

She clutched the rail as the ship dipped suddenly into the steep trough of a wave. The captain, it occurred to Night, was wise in heading for shore in the *Johanna Jones* herself instead of sending the passengers back by motorboat. What frightened fools the other passengers must be to huddle together inside, away from this marvelous display. She threw her head back and raised an arm to the sky.

A wave slowly lifted over the gunwale, rose higher and higher until it towered above her, and suddenly broke, crashing and roaring, as it covered her with icy salt water. Night plunged to the deck and was lifted and swept along. Choking, squirming she was borne down the cold chute, arms and legs battering against walls. Steadying himself against a wall, Norris seized her and thrust her down the stairs. He came down after her, found a lantern, lit it and then helped Night get up.

Stunned and wet, she stood against the wall staring at him. She didn't seem to recognize him. Her hair was loose and wet. Her dress clung to her. As Norris watched, she danced a slow, involuntary dance to keep from falling: a long forward step as the ship lurched to port, a step or two to either side, and a quick recovery back to the wall. She did this a few times, almost unconsciously, and then, in a tone amazingly steady, she finally said:

"What's happened to the ship?" But before Norris could answer, she added, "Oh, you're Stoner Young, the new attorney. Out here." Norris nodded.

"I'll have to make a try at steering this hulk," he told her gravely. "I have a feeling she's deserted. The captain's drunk or dead to let her go on like this."

The ship lurched, throwing them violently against the wall.

"Well for God's sakes do it! Do it!" She yelled, suddenly terrified. "Steer it!"

Norris found a ladder near the passageway and climbed it. He went up two more ladders and then he was on the bridge. Part of the bridge had already been torn away. He went inside and took hold of the wheel. With a sharp vicious motion it flipped him to the floor. He stayed there. His right temple started to bleed. Over him, the wheel moved gently by itself. Norris lay on the floor, breathing heavily, conscious of nothing....

CHAPTER TWENTY-FOUR

A SQUAT, moist three feet of madness rolled onto the heaving deck. As Hymie thrust himself along on his casters, he felt accomplishment and consummation big in him. The storm had become a snarling mob of winds rushing low across the ocean. It made hideous sounds. But the sounds could not obliterate the vision of the legs. The vision had become a frenzied obsession. He had to have those legs. He started out to get them. So certain was he that they were already his that he felt no need to hurry.

He went to a store room amidships. As he entered, the ship dove and Hymie was thrown against an empty gun rack. He hurled himself back, uncomplainingly, upon his wheeled platform. Because it was dark he had trouble finding what he was after. The ship bumped and pitched him. Braced against the gun rack, he extended a hand behind it and found what he sought. It was a long-bladed knife with a strong, short shaft; he slid it from its sheath and felt its blade. Keen as a new-honed razor! It would be a good knife, Hymie considered complacently, with which to cut off a pair of legs … a wonderful pair of legs whose constant threat of moving away, because of some whim of the creature upon them, was vastly annoying.

Hymie tucked the knife under his stumps. It felt good, there. He was calmer now, with the steady calm of controlled energy. Also, he knew now what everything was about. All things were made plain. Never, it seemed to Hymie, had he had less need of explanations. His course lay straight before him. The terrible clarity, the false lucidity of the paranoiac was his. The reasons for all acts and all needs were made brilliantly clear. He knew why Stoner Young had agreed to defend him, knew why that Haldorn had been killed, knew all there was to know of significance in the world....

He heard the babble of voices and he peered about, astonished. Men and women chattered around him, but he could see nothing.

"Shut up!" Hymie Gold screamed. The babbling continued; evidently they couldn't hear him. He waited and finally the voices faded.

Through the crack between the doors he could see a thin line of yellow light. Hymie pushed the doors apart and slid in on silent wheels.

Underneath a table he saw the legs. The table hid the rest of the woman's body. For Hymie the world stopped right there. The legs were outlined by a dress of glossy black; under the light that flowed down from the table they seemed more delectable than ever. Hymie's joy was so great he found breathing difficult. The legs belonged to the widow of the man whose death got Hymie into trouble. Now the legs would be his. The babble of invisible voices died out altogether. Hymie was left alone in an enormous, empty silence.

He had to give voice, in some small measure, to what seethed in him. There was too much of it for him longer to contain. The pot boiled over. "A-ah A-aah." His breath poured out in a harsh ecstatic moan. At this, the legs moved.

Hymie remembered giving the jewels to the woman on the legs. He was of no mind to hurry things. How sweetly anticipation ran in him.

"Go away," Night said. Her voice was cold and brittle. Hymie looked at her dumbly. The words had no meaning. He waggled his head sharply as if to shake off the two words. Night backed away, holding her hands out in front of her. Incoherent sounds fell from her lips. She saw Hymie Gold with a gun in one hand, a long knife in the other, and a pair of eyes glinting with madness. Hymie watched her warily. But when hysteria seized her and she laughed wildly, the sound disturbed him.

"I'll tell you something, baby ..." he said. His throat was thick with saliva. Talking, he found, was exceedingly difficult to manage.

The sea chose that instant to draw the *Johanna Jones* back on her stern, like an arrow on a taut bow; abruptly released, the old boat flung forward, sweeping over the turbulent sea. The salon crumpled, a card house in a storm. Everything in it flew. Night, standing rigid with fright, was thrown to the top of the bar from where she rolled senseless to the floor. Hymie went sliding across the floor, too heavy to be jerked free. And he marked, as he moved, how the girl's body fell. He was sure he knew just where it lay behind the bar, under black satin and white velvet.

The knife was in his hand. Where his fingers stopped and the knife began, he could not tell. The knife and his hand were one.

Joy swirled about him as he rolled across the floor to the bar. The ship groaned, listing heavily; she was down by the bow. The sea slapped her like a bear cuffing a cub, side to side. Vast breakers pounded her toward the rocks of the cape. The wheels of Hymie's platform clicked across a crack as they took him around the bar. The list of the ship let him lean comfortably against the wall and roll along without effort. He had a gun in his other hand.

There they were. He made out the splotch of white that was her jacket, first. Dimly he saw it rise and fall with her breathing. And gradually, as he stared, the outlines of the legs emerged, sheathed in the dark satin. He felt the flesh under the cloth. The head of the woman was hidden from him, under the bar. He put his gun against the white mark where he thought the heart ought to be, and fired until the gun was empty. There were eight shots. At the first one, a convulsive stir had jerked through her. Then she had been still.

As he cut through the flesh with his knife he felt the blood flow warm over his hands. Why bother to take the gown off the legs? The knife tore crisply through the cloth to the skin, softly through the flesh, and stopped at the bone. He snapped the bone at the hips. Hoarse sighs of animal pleasure escaped him as he felt the blade separate flesh from flesh. He trembled with joy. His cheek itched and he stopped to scratch it. He wiped his hand under his armpit before he started to sever the other leg. He was careful not to let his blade touch the thigh. He began to hack at a muscle that refused to part. It parted. His soft hands grubbed in viscera soapy with blood. The vertebra broke under his fist. The legs were free of the body.

He drew his awful prize away, turned, and rolled across the room clasping the legs under one arm as the other pushed him along.

The sky lighted up again as Hymie moved onto the deck. The vivid flash revealed Hymie carrying the trousered legs of Devlin Kurtz. Thick hair glistened bloodily where the legs were uncovered.

When Hymie came to his own quarters, he left it dark. His satisfaction was in touch, not sight....

Rain came at last, flaying the ship with whips of cold water. The sea hammered her toward the jagged nose of Cape Todos Santos.

CHAPTER TWENTY-FIVE

D AWN of the next day, as it spread over the coastal hills, lit up a calm world of blue sea and brown shore. Fast-falling water had washed the air clear. A phalanx of ashen seagulls split the even line of its flight and circled down to inspect the *Johanna Jones.* The gulls coasted, glided on still wings, hovered over her, cawing, searching her decks and the waters around her for food. At length they soared up again and fled along to the south.

The old hulk clung to the spear of rock upon which she was impaled, a dying man refusing to let a saber be withdrawn from his body. She had come a long and violent way to this haven. The sea had washed away all wreckage, and above water there were no wounds on her white body except forward to port where a section of railing had been torn away.

Royla moved out of the companionway and stood at the rail. Rage confused her. She swayed and clung to the rail. There was something she had to do. She went across the sun-flooded deck and down in the gloom to Hymie's bed-chamber.

He lay asleep on the couch, uncovered. In each hand he clutched a stiff and bloody leg. Blood spattered him, crusty and dry. One red scab of it shone grotesquely over his right cheekbone.

He was entirely limp when Royla lifted him upon the comfortably concave seat of his splendid marble limbs and set the minute steel clamps that locked him securely into place. His big head gangled over on his shoulder. His limp fingers relaxed and the dead stumps fell to the floor. Royla hurried. The atmosphere here sickened her.

She caught up a silvered thermos bottle of iced water from its swinging rack, unstoppered it and flung the water across Hymie's face. He did not move. Again she drenched him. This time his head jerked upright and his eyelids rolled, bewildered. He sputtered. Words stuck in his throat.

He recognized Royla and anger flared across his face. He tried to shout. No sound came.

Royla wheeled him out on deck. Finally his throat cleared and he began to roar at her, cursing horribly. His hands clawed her and drew blood; they ripped her dress over her shoulder blades. She was bent low, pushing the stone legs along; Hymie's nails drew deep scarlet lines on her skin. He struck at her head. Royla, heedless, continued to push. The casters clicked across the boards as they rolled. Hymie screamed. Royla began to move faster.

When she had brought him to the edge of the deck where the railing was gone, she stopped.

"This," Royla said, panting, "is the end of you. You're going to hell to rot."

She lunged at the pedestal. It tipped, hovered, fell back heavily. Royla hurled herself forward again. The thing that was half Hymie and half stone tilted out over the water. Hymie screamed a high, terrible scream, jagged with terror. His arms waved. The figure righted itself in the air as the heavy legs swung into plumb, striking the water with a loud splash.

Royla leaned over the edge of the deck and stared, fascinated.

Deep, deep down below she saw something flash as it reflected the sun. She had a final glimpse of writhing arms, and then everything went dark. Clusters of bubbles broke the surface of the water rocking over the expanding circles made by the crash.

Royla spat and turned away.

CHAPTER TWENTY-SIX

SETTLED on the veranda of the Casa del Caballo Blanco, the dusty and uncomfortable wooden box that was the only lodging place in Iglesia, Norris Haldorn felt that everything was now clear before him. The riddle was solved. He was going back to the Irrawaddy ...

He was seated on a bench that stuck out from the wall of the hotel like a shelf; trouser seats sliding across it had polished the plank to a high brown gloss. Spread out before him lay a curve of baking land, shimmering under the fierce blue of the Mexican sky. Yes, he was going back to Burma; he knew at last what there was for him to do.

Señor Vicente y Torrano moved out into the sun, near Norris. A small, thin woman with a pinched hard face hurried out behind him with a wide, floppy wicker chair. He sank panting into it. Even the tuberculars came no more to Iglesia, he complained, in Spanish.

"The hundred miles between here and Todos Santos is the dryest and hottest plateau in the continent," he told Norris. "It is high, too. And mine is the only hotel in all this wonderful land for the cure of all the ailments and diseases of the lungs." His head wobbled dolefully. "Dryest and hottest and very high," he repeated in his smooth voice.

"I would not argue with you on that score," Norris said. "I don't believe anybody would." In the two weeks since he had tottered into Iglesia, blind with thirst, carrying Night, his Spanish had come back to him. He talked easily with Señor Vicente y Torrano.

"Another week and your wife will be strong enough for the journey," the fat man announced in the manner of a physician. He stroked his sweaty chin. "Yes, yes; another three days."

"How long ought the trip to take?" Norris asked.

The question angered Vicente y Torrano. He lifted both his big feet and slapped them down against the boards of the porch.

"That damned stage company! There are no passengers for two, three weeks and what do they do? They abandon the service. No more autos to Iglesia. How are sick people to come here and be cured if no one will carry them? It is cruelty. It is a sin they have committed. Swine, those stage people. Do they have any patience? Do they have any faith? No ! Twice no, and damn them!"

"There must have been some activity in oil here at one time." Norris had seen a derrick at the end of the dribble of shacks that marked Iglesia's street.

"That was it," Vicente y Torrano admitted ruefully. His brother had sold him the ranch seven years before when the oil had been found. And the oil was still there, but it would take three, four, five—he did not know just how many hundreds of miles of pipe line to get it to the refinery and the terminals. And the big companies wouldn't deal with him. He had built the Casa del Caballo Blanco—he waved an arm proudly—and about those first years he would not now complain. From the ranch there had come plenty for them to eat and from the guests enough money to buy some luxuries. "In that time I had one fine automobile, and now I have this aged Ford," he said sadly. Business had declined. And now, with this damned stage company refusing service altogether, a man might as well give it all up....

One of his daughters—he had eight—turned the corner of the building and climbed up into the shade to sit, bare brown legs swinging, on the edge of the porch. She was as small and uncurved and ugly as her mother, but she had such skin as Norris had never seen before. It had a dry, silky sheen, and was the color of new chamois. Casually, without turning her head, she said to her father, "The gasoline is all gone. Evaporated. *Tenemos nada.*"

Vicente y Torrano sputtered and choked, moving up and down in a slow kind of bounce in his wobbly chair. When he appeared to have calmed, the girl said, "Your own fault, papa. You left the top of the tank open. I looked in a few minutes ago and it's bone dry." She went on swinging her legs, out and back, out and back, out and back....

"Then you and your wife must go by the horsecarriage," Vicente y Torrano announced.

"They can't do that, either," the girl informed him placidly.

"No? No? Can't go by the carriage?"

"No, papa," she insisted patiently, "The spokes have cracked in the wheels and two have sprung out of the rim. The carriage will not run at all."

His defeat complete, her father fell back, held his face in his hand, let his mouth slide open, and sighed profoundly. There was nothing, then. No way out. And nothing left to poor, poor Alfredo Vicente y Torrano. *Pobre Alfredo.* The guests must remain. He had planned his best and God had seen fit to thwart him. No man could resist the will of Heaven. He thought of the present the gentleman had promised him as soon as he and his wife should be safely back at their home in the United States.

"How about going on horseback?" Norris asked.

"You'd die," the girl said stolidly. "As soon as you get beyond that rim there and you go up, the heat gets much worse than here, even at night. It comes right up out of the canyons at night as if it had hid there all day and waited for dark."

It was on the edge of just such a canyon that the woman Royla had died in that terrible trip from the tip of Todos Santos across the Baja California bad lands to Iglesia, Norris remembered. Who or what she was he hadn't known, but she had left the wrecked *Johanna Jones* with Night and him, a disheveled, silent creature, bearing hideous scratches on her face. She had died in the same silent way and her face, terrible, festering, stood sickeningly clear in Norris' memory. On the second day they had used the last of the water brought with them from the ship, and they had had to strike inland away from the endless glittering brown beach in search of a spring or a stream. They hadn't found any. The weight of Night's limp body across his back, over his shoulder,—he could feel it even now.

"But why, if it's safe in a carriage, isn't it safe to go on horseback?" he asked the girl, who had drawn up her legs and coiled herself upon the porch.

"Maybe safe for you," she conceded, "but for your wife—no." Her voice was scornful. "She could not ride ten miles, from the looks of her. With a soft behind like hers, she would die of the saddle pain before one day was over. It is hard riding. And papa's horses are not easy seats," she finished boldly.

Vicente y Torrano made no move to contradict her comment on his horses. The girl reared herself on the palms of her hands and inspected her father's face. He was sleeping.

"Even for me, I would not make that ride on one of our horses," the girl went on. "And I have been riding out here all my life." Norris wondered if she could be more than fourteen or fifteen. "The carriage is not broken, Señor Haldorn. The wheels are all right, and the spokes are not cracked. I told that to papa so he would not try to send you in it. I like you. It would be bad for you to go in that carriage. Better for you to stay here and rest until an automobile comes. Maybe the stage or some soldiers or some tourists. Some one will come sometime."

Norris saw that his host slept and asked, "Won't he go round and look at the carriage himself?"

"Papa! *Look himself?* Papa?" She giggled and held her face up. "I tell you this,—if my mother would not bring the chair behind him, he would sleep on the boards. He looks for nothing."

Norris sat absolutely still. To move a hand required tremendous effort in this heat. It would be years, he supposed, before the effects of the complete drying-out his body had undergone would disappear. A heavy lassitude settled over him. He wilted into a kind of mild stupor of exhaustion. The girl watched his face, a strange merger of gaunt weariness and glowing sunburn ...

Weeks during which he drowsed at the Casa del Caballo Blanco slid along quietly, unmarked, without event.

Night Gambier left the hostelry of Señor Vicente y Torrano in the car of a group of archaeologists, under federal escort, headed south. Three days later she was at the border and on a train headed for El Paso.

CHAPTER TWENTY-SEVEN

T HE air had the tule fog smell, less sharp than the smell of sea fog. And it smelled of coal smoke and cinders. Norris walked out of the arcade of the Third and Townsend Station in San Francisco.

He stood back against a pile of trunks by the gray wall of the station to let a crowd of commuters go by in a murmurous rush. Some of them were reading books, taking their direction by the feel of the bodies in front of them. He could hear, behind the wall, the clanging of train bells.

There was no reason to hurry. He knew just what he was going to do. From here he was going on to Shanghai, around the China Sea and up to Burma, to the girl Narapatee and the greatest happiness he had ever known.

It might be interesting, now that there was no necessity to press his actions, to visit McMoyle again and discover what, if anything, the police had determined regarding the death of Ed Blackburn. His interest remained a mild, unperturbed kind of curiosity. He no longer cared about the restoration of his identity. He walked up on the cobbles of Townsend street. A monstrous truck, set low to the ground, like a packing box on spools, pulled by a team of stubby horses, rolled along beside him with a comfortable clapping noise. It didn't matter who he was. Peace and happiness, that was all that mattered.

He passed a stable and saw horses still inside, and rows of oily black leather collars and straps hanging on pegs. A dog was asleep with his nose between his paws on the floor.

He would have to have some more money. He only had two hundred and nine dollars. Night would give him enough to carry him where he had to go.

At the corner, a baldheaded man shouted from the back of a small truck placarded with religious posters. A crowd had collected. Norris didn't want to shoulder through the mass. He took a hack taxi at the curb and told the driver to take him to police headquarters. After that, he planned, he'd obtain the money he needed and complete his other arrangements.

A half hour later Norris was eating in Tadisch's with two detectives. They had insisted, with fierce cordiality, that he accompany them to the table. Before that, they had told him McMoyle wasn't in, and had shown him around the building. They had dallied in the shooting gallery in the basement and fingered guns and put them into Norris' hand and taken them out again, and had shown him the identification bureau and the show-up theater. McMoyle would be glad to see him. McMoyle would be back, they said, any minute now.

"We'll go back now, if you're ready," Norris said. The police couldn't have hit upon anything vital in the case because these men would have known it, he reasoned. The detectives were being bovinely mysterious. Norris grew tired of it suddenly. One was on each side of him, walking along Sacramento street, past the Chinese jewelry shops, windows full of bright yellow Chinese gold and splinters of jade. "What kind of a damned fool joke is this?" he demanded.

They seized him, one to an arm. "This isn't a joke, Young. You're going to see McMoyle all right." He wrenched free. When they made to grasp his sleeves again, he struck sharply. His blow caught the detective on the side of the nose and the man sprawled. His companion smashed his fist, encased in the steel ring of a handcuff, against the side of Norris' jaw.

An hour later he was sitting in a cell in the city prison, charged with the murder of Norris Haldorn.

Downstairs, the detective bureau received cigars and congratulations from the chief after he had examined two sets of fingerprints.

"And to think," McMoyle chuckled, standing feet apart, hands in his trouser pockets, "that he walked in here on us asking for information. It's either a case of a million dollars worth of gall or else the guy thought that would be a cute way to kill suspicion. But on that insanity end of it—"

The chief interrupted, "Have you got anything beyond the fingerprints? And you're sure you're clear on motive?"

McMoyle had to admit that the fingerprints, with the gun, composed the major prosecution evidence. "But," he assured the chief, "he can't prove any alibi. He can't tell us where he was that night. And what's more—what I was just going to tell you—he pops out to Danny and Allen here that he's Norris Haldorn. Can you tie that? Says *he's* Norris Haldorn. My God, that's a funny one. He thinks he's the guy he bumped off. That really does sound nuts, know that?"

The chief grinned, "Yeah? Pretty smart nuts, I'd say. How does he explain the stuff we've got on him?"

"He doesn't," McMoyle said eagerly. "No sir, he doesn't. Just sniffs at that and says he's going to bring the whole thing out into the open, whatever that means."

"Sounds to me like he's getting ready for a real hot insanity defense already." The chief rubbed his cheek with the eraser on his pencil. "If he's that kind, let him alone, see? When they make plans for a trial this far ahead, it means their nerves are going to crack. I know. No visitors. Tell them he's sick or sleeping. No 'phone calls. And no attorney in to see him before a week. Get that, now. You guys have done pretty damned good in this business. I got to say it."

The room swam in slow blue smoke.

CHAPTER TWENTY-EIGHT

"Y OU do solemnly swear to tell the truth, the whole truth and nothing b' the truth, s'help you God?"

"I do."

"Be seated please. Right up there beside the judge."

"What is your name?"

"Mrs. Norris Haldorn."

"And you are the widow of the deceased in this case?"

"Y-yes, I am."

"Have you ever seen the defendant in this case, Stoner Young, prior to seeing him in court?"

"Yes, I have. It was on the—"

"Please don't volunteer information, Mrs. Haldorn. Just answer my questions and let me conduct the defense. Mrs. Haldorn, have you a good memory?"

"Just a moment—objected as calling for conclusion of the witness."

"Overruled. Let it go, Mr. District Attorney. Let your opponent lay his groundwork, anyway."

"Answer the question, Mrs. Haldorn."

"Have I a good memory? Why, yes; I have."

"And you have heard the witnesses for the prosecution give their testimony, have you?"

"I have."

"You have been in court, have you not, every day of this trial except the first three days during which the jury was being chosen and no testimony was given?"

"Will counsel separate his questions?"

"Very well, very well. Mrs. Haldorn, you have been in court ever since the fourth day of this trial, in constant attendance, haven't you?"

"Yes, that's true."

"Now then; you heard the prosecution witness—it was Dr. Heinrichs—you heard him testify that the fingerprints found upon the gun were the—"

"Objected to on the ground the gun is not properly identified."

"Not identified? Are you objecting to testimony on your own side of the fence? This is becoming farcical."

"If it is, then you are responsible."

"Are you trying to tell me how to practice law?"

"Gentlemen, gentlemen! I shall have to direct counsel to end this bickering. I will determine when this trial is farcical and when it is not. Objection sustained. Gun wasn't properly identified. Continue."

"All right, all right; I'll identify the gun for the District Attorney. It is the gun already in evidence marked State's exhibit number—what is the number of that exhibit, Clerk? Forty-three? The State's exhibit number forty-three. It is the gun alleged to have discharged the bullet that ended the life of Norris Haldorn. Now, Mrs. Haldorn, you heard the witness, Dr. Heinrichs, say that the fingerprints on that pistol—gun, I mean—were fingerprints coinciding with those of the defendant. You heard that testimony, did you not?"

"Yes, I heard it, yes that's right."

"All right. You also heard the prosecution witnesses, I mean the police officers, that is, testify regarding certain conversations they had with the defendant, Mr. Young. I refer now to the conversations in which they claimed Mr. Young told them he could not remember where he was upon the day the death of your husband occurred."

"Yes, I heard that testimony."

"And you also listened when the other prosecution witnesses—and now I refer to the two detectives, Allen Menas and Daniel Carborale—you listened when they sat on the stand and said under oath that the defendant informed them that he was himself, in fact, Norris Haldorn? You heard that, didn't you, Mrs. Haldorn?"

"Yes, I did."

"You also heard those same two detectives, without naming them again, testify regarding certain alleged peculiar conduct on the part of the defendant, and heard them further testify, or admit, in answer to questions, that they had publicly stated the defendant would claim to be insane, and heard them further testify that they publicly stated they considered him goofy, to use their own words?"

"Yes, sir."

"Counsel, what is the purpose of this resume? It is conceded the witness has been present and that she heard all of the testimony. Why prolong this? I can't see where it's leading you."

"If your Honor please, I am laying the basis for a general question. I want to establish the competency of—Will Your Honor bear with me a moment while I confer with my client? ... (Whispers). Mr. Young, it's absolute suicide to do what you want. I simply can't ask this woman if she believes her husband was Norris Haldorn. I *can't* do it, man, I tell you. Nobody in the world thinks for an instant he wasn't Haldorn, except you. And it doesn't make any difference if he was the Prince of Wales. His name doesn't matter. It's the *man*, the human being, that you're accused of murdering, not the name."

"And I tell you to ask her that question. You feel sure of her answer. I think she'll break."

"Let's not argue that again here in the courtroom. She's already said she was the widow of Norris Haldorn."

"Damn it, do as I tell you!"

"But, Mr. Young, it will ruin you with the jury."

"Counsel."

"Ruin, hell! It's my life that's on trial, not yours."

"Counsel—"

"Yes, Your Honor?"

"I am speaking to you also, Mr. District Attorney. The witness has spoken to me while the defense attorney was conferring privately with his client. I have heard what she had to say. I believe she should speak now. I have given her permission to volunteer information. I will put it in the form of a question from the Court. Mrs. Haldorn, you have something further, something relevant to add to your testimony, have you not? Will you add it?"

"I have made up my mind to tell—to tell all I know about my husband's death. He … he committed suicide. He—"

"What? My God, what was that? What—"

"Did you hear that? She said—"

"Jeeze, let me get to a 'phone, I got a deadline—"

"That's the widow and she said—"

"Quiet! Quiet, I say! This is a court of law. We must have decorum here. Let the witness proceed. Counsel, keep your objections until later; until the witness has finished. You can move to strike out, then. Mr. District Attorney, please be seated and control yourself, I say. You may not enter any objection now. I will not entertain it. Let the record show you objected to my ruling. Continue, Mrs. Haldorn."

"But, Your Honor—"

"Be *seated!* Continue, Mrs. Haldorn."

"That's all true. He killed himself. As God is my judge, I am telling the truth. I know my husband took his own life. Stoner Young did not kill him. At the moment Norris Haldorn killed himself, Stoner Young was with me. He was with me the whole evening. I'm going to tell all the truth. He was with me the whole night. We stayed together. I swear it. It's true. I swear before God it's true. I'm going to tell how the whole thing happened now. I don't care any longer.... They say Norris died about midnight. I spoke to him on the telephone at fifteen minutes to twelve and he told me he was going to kill himself. I didn't believe him. I told him I didn't care what he did. He called me pet names. Then he said it didn't matter if I cared or not, that he just wanted me to know he was going to shoot himself. I didn't know where he was telephoning from. Somewhere in the city, he said. I was in our home in Hillsborough. I can prove that. This is the God's honest truth.... Stoner Young was there all the time. He was with me until ten o'clock the next morning ... I have kept this inside me but I can't keep it any longer.... No, no, no ... I can't ... He's not guilty, I tell you.... That's why he says he can't remember where he was. He was with me ... Saying it for me ... For me ... Oh, please ..."

"Court stands adjourned for ten minutes. Will the bailiff help the witness from the stand."

"Just a moment, Your Honor. I object to this adjournment. I won't have the jury retiring like this, and all. I won't. This is amazing!"

"Mr. District Attorney, it makes no difference what you will or will not have. The Court has ruled. That is final."

"I desire to object with all my power and every bit of authority the people vest in me as their prosecutor against this adjournment. I want an opportunity here and now to examine this woman on the stand and to re-examine after the cross. In the name of the people of the State of California, I demand it. There must be no adjournment. I know what that means. A conference and a refusal to testify again, or a collapse so I can't get at her. I know. I know, I tell you."

"Your Honor, I ask that counsel be reprimanded for those statements and that—"

"Will Your Honor entertain a motion to permit only the jury and the witness to retire and require the defendant and his counsel to remain seated in the courtroom?"

"I will not entertain such a motion. Court is adjourned. The jury will retire."

"Mr. District Attorney, you may take the witness. Oh, just a minute. That is right. She is a defense witness. The direct is not finished yet. Counsel for the Defense, have you finished with this witness?"

"Yes, Your Honor. We have no further questions."

"Now, Mr. Prosecutor, go ahead."

"The State has some very vital questions to ask Mrs. Haldorn."

"Proceed, Counsel."

"Mrs. Haldorn, when you knew this story all the time, this story you claim is the truth, why did you keep silent until now, knowing that if you were ill or kept in some way from testifying it might mean the death of a man you believed to be innocent? Why, I ask you?"

"Because I was sure Mr. Young would be acquitted without my testimony. I became fearful today and decided to—to disobey him and tell the truth."

"I see. You decided to disobey Mr. Young. You mean the Mr. Stoner Young accused of murdering your husband, don't you?"

"Yes, I mean Mr. Young."

"I see. Hm. And how long before the murder of your husband, Mrs. Haldorn had you been maintaining a liaison with Mr. Stoner Young?"

"Your Honor, we object to that as improper cross-examination, assuming something not in evidence and object to it on the further ground that it is incompetent, irrelevant and immaterial."

"Overruled. The question will be allowed. Will you please answer it, Mrs. Haldorn."

"If you want me to state how long I had known Mr. Young I will say four years."

"That is not what I asked, Mrs. Haldorn. I want to know for how long before the murder of your husband you had sexual intercourse with Stoner Young, the defendant in this case?"

"Your Honor, we renew our objection."

"Overruled. Let the record show you excepted. Answer, Mrs. Haldorn."

"For two days.... Oh, my God...."

"Jeeze, she's fainted!"

"Boy, there's my home edition headline."

"I have no further questions on behalf of the State, Your Honor. I wish to announce that this office intends to make a full investigation of the activities and movements of Mrs. Haldorn on the day and night of her husband's murder, in consideration of the admissions she has made here today and furthermore that—"

"Stop! Your Honor, we ask that you admonish counsel at once. He is attempting to influence the jury. It is all wrong."

"There is no need, Your Honor. The State's remarks are concluded."

"Counsel, did you have a motion?"

"Yes. The defense moves at this time for a directed verdict of not guilty. We move the Court that the Court advise and instruct the jury to return a verdict of not guilty. I believe the evidence clearly shows a great consistency with the innocence of the defendant and that any evidence tending to show guilt on the part of the defendant is far outweighed by the evidence proving his innocence. The State has not proved its case."

"Just a moment; there is no need to argue the motion. It was superfluous. The Court was about to instruct the jury. The motion is granted and—"

"But, Your Honor, the State objects. This is all very irregular and the case is not all in yet."

"Not all in? Have you any further witnesses?"

"No, we have not, it is true."

"Are there any further witnesses for the defense?"

"No, Your Honor."

"Then there is no necessity for wasting time—with futile examination of witnesses who have already testified."

"But I submit, Your Honor, that there has been no corroborative evidence. It is this woman's unsupported statement and she has admitted a strong personal interest in the defendant."

"Corroboration? Since when is the burden on the defense, Mr. District Attorney? I will not descend to arguing with counsel. Have you or have you not any new testimony, or any testimony or evidence at all to rebut that given by Mrs. Haldorn?"

"No, I haven't but—"

"Then let that end it. I will instruct the jury to find the defendant not guilty of the charge. Mr. Clerk, hand me my glasses."

"But, but—but Your Honor—I'll charge them both with conspiracy. That woman—look at the interest she has in this case."

"Charge as you please, Mr. District Attorney. I am conducting this court and I will administer the law and let the jury determine the facts when there are facts to determine. There can be no dispute here."

"Your Honor, this is an outrage to the people of the State."

"No, it is not an outrage, Mr. District Attorney; it is simple justice."

CHAPTER TWENTY-NINE

NORRIS was climbing up Clay street past the neat, steep lawns and palm clusters of Lafayette Park. It was his last day in San Francisco. Possibly, he reflected, his last in America. On the other side of the street, covering the corner, was the tattered ruin of an old clapboard home, four stories high, painted with sand so that it glittered in the sun. A good many of the older houses had sand in their paint like that. Everything about this one was ornate, fussy, disintegrating. Boards covered some of the broken windows. Cupolas stuck out all over the place. With all its ugly wooden embroidery, it had probably been considered a marvel of beauty when it had been built. At that time, no doubt, it had had a name. It had been "the Guerrero house" or "the Maraschi house," as he, too, Norris remembered, had been an important name.

To his right a narrow path covered with red rock crystals led at a steep angle up to the crest of the little park; from there, Norris knew, he would be able to look down and away to the north, to San Rafael and to Richmond with its clusters of white oil tanks, and to the pale dots that were the Farallones. He ought to have had, he thought now, a faithful servant who would appear out of the past and identify him, in spite of his scars, in spite of his changed voice. Hymie Gold could have proved that Blackburn was an impostor. Norris wondered why he hadn't done so.

But it didn't really matter. The yacht was his again. Night Gambier had given it to him. In it, he was going to Burma. Eight months had passed since he had left that land, but it seemed like eight times eight years. It was somehow comforting to remember that the interval was so short, that he might return and find nothing changed, nothing gone. In that thought lay a good measure of solace.

In the enclosure on top of the hill there was a single bench of boards, painted bright green and held up by legs of iron. He sat down. The air up here was clearer; all the shining terraces and gardens and blue bay and green sea and brown hills spreading out before him appeared curiously close. He had the peak of the park here to himself. He felt old and very tired. Almost too tired to go on to that unrevealed and alluring future.

From the apple-green bush, part of the hedge that fenced the crest of the park, he pulled a handful of brittle leaves and crushed them in his palm; they smelled of lemons, tart and crisp with sap. Not a sound reached him here. The sun poured down, filling him with a warm serenity. Below, lawns went steeply down to streets and streets hurried still more steeply to the coves of sail-speckled Yacht Harbor. So still as to seem without life, utterly abandoned, clumps of apartment houses, high and thin, stood on Nob Hill and Russian Hill.

The crunch of shoes stepping along the gravel warned him someone else had come and he stood up to leave; the peace he found here could not contain two. It would lose its deep and rich tranquillity.

A woman stood by the bench, her hands, encased in gloves of pale gray silk, resting on the back board.

"I would like to talk to you," Night said.

He sat down with her. He had meant to see her anyhow, before leaving. He wanted to talk to her about the trial, especially about its ending.

Examining her now in his unhurried, meditative way, he thought he marked a certain austerity in her face. Not stiffness, precisely, nor coldness, but reserve. As he watched, it was gone.

"I wanted to tell you why I did it," she announced clamly. "Why I testified, I mean. Why I said what I did in court."

Suddenly he did not care to know. "You don't have to tell me," he said steadily.

"I'm afraid it's necessary," Night answered, gently. "You saved my life."

"Well, God knows you saved mine. And I know it. I think that makes us even."

The woman relaxed. Her hands, which had been tensely gripping the edge of the bench, let go and fondled each other gently in her lap. "It cost thirty thousand dollars to square that judge beforehand. He knew I was lying."

"I wondered how much you had to pay him. More than I thought, at that."

Night continued. "There's one more thing. I hope—hope you'll bear with me if I get nervous telling it. It's this: When Norris was shot he was talking on the telephone. You remember about that. Talking to that Hymie Gold." Mention of the name did not perturb her. "I want to repeat to you what Hymie Gold told me. You know. He told me this on that terrible night on the ship when he was squatting there with a knife in his hand. Just before the wreck that saved me. Hymie Gold told me the words Norris spoke just before he was shot, the words that came over the telephone. I can't understand what they mean. There's something frightful about them."

"Well," Norris said, "what were they? Let's have it."

"He said that as Norris was shot, he heard him scream out, 'Oh, Jesus Christ, it's Haldorn come back! Let me alone!'"

Norris stood up. Far inside him something flamed. He went over the words again. Hymie Gold had heard Ed Blackburn scream them as he was murdered. Scream them. And Norris slid back in his memory to a bleakly blank place....

Night was staring anxiously at him. He turned and sank slowly to the bench again.

"I've heard those words before," he said heavily, deliberately. "Yes, I recall now that I heard them. ... It was the day I came to San Francisco ... but I don't remember what happened ... I woke up in some lodging house ... I was sick."

Night raised a trembling hand to her forehead. He reached up for the hand, clasped it between both of his and brought it back slowly to her lap. "I was sick, I tell you." His fingers tightened his hold. "Can't you see now!"

She whispered, "No."

He felt that the past was a scarlet thread that had just been cut....

"Let's drop it then...." He moved a pebble impatiently with the toe of his shoe. "Let's not talk about it any more." He released her hand; she patted his, laughing weakly.

"As you like. I'd need to be a clairvoyant to understand you."

"A clairvoyant?" he echoed dully. "Sometimes I am...." He saw Blackburn and Night together on the yacht in Burma ... they were wearing shackles ... his shackles ... and then, without really understanding, he realized that he had freed them both.

"Let's stop," she said. "We're both babbling nonsense." There was a long silence.

"Good-bye," Norris said finally, rising. Night nodded.

Norris went slowly down the hill, down the path strewn with little maroon stones, down toward the shadowed walk under the walls. Night sat on the bench and stared, puzzled, at the patterns in yellow lace spun by the sun on the ground in front of the glossy green hedges.

For Norris, the whole world, and all that was past, and the mysterious future ahead, had miraculously been caparisoned with justice and jewelled with hopes bright and alluring. And he was going back to the smoky-yellow Irrawaddy and up to hot Paok-to in quest of the girl Narapatee.

A peddler on a wagon behind a sleepy horse was at the curb. The peddler held up a bag of fruit. Norris gave him a coin for it.

"There ain't nobody pays much attention nowadays to a man alone trying to get along," the peddler complained. "This is the first sale I've made today. It's a rotten mean world. Rotten mean, I can tell you."

"Old man," Norris said slowly, joyfully, "old man, you're a liar."

THE END.

www.ingramcontent.com/pod-product-compliance
Lightning Source LLC
Chambersburg PA
CBHW031230260626
47169CB00007B/2238